Oliver Bell Bunce

Bachelor Bluff

His Opinions, Sentiments, and Disputations

Oliver Bell Bunce

Bachelor Bluff
His Opinions, Sentiments, and Disputations

ISBN/EAN: 9783744652490

Printed in Europe, USA, Canada, Australia, Japan

Cover: Foto ©Raphael Reischuk / pixelio.de

More available books at **www.hansebooks.com**

BACHELOR BLUFF:

HIS OPINIONS, SENTIMENTS, AND DISPUTATIONS.

BY

OLIVER BELL BUNCE.

NEW YORK:
D. APPLETON AND COMPANY,
1, 3, AND 5 BOND STREET.
1881.

HABITUAL readers of "Appletons' Journal," who may chance upon this volume, will find in it many things with which they are already familiar ; but they will also discover that many changes have been made — that with a few exceptions the material has been rearranged, extended, newly combined, and otherwise considerably altered. There are indisputably numerous old pieces in the patchwork, but the fresh combinations make the patterns almost new.

"*REMEMBER*," said Bachelor Bluff, "*that Truth commonly goes in russet and Error in purple. The sober judgment which can not be seduced by the glitter of false ideas hides itself in by-ways among slow, humdrum people, while Error envelops itself in alluring sophistries that captivate brilliant men and women. Do not deny this until you have well thought of it, and then you will not deny it.*"

"*HAVE I BORROWED!*" exclaimed the Bachelor. "*From everything and everywhere, to the best of my ability; from life in its varied forms, and from those open reservoirs of stolen learning called books. He is richest in this world who borrows most. Let all men be intellectual highwaymen, waylaying ideas everywhere, appropriating facts in all directions, and plundering every circumstance of its significant meaning.*"

"*WHAT IS TO BE LEARNED! Whether a man learns or not, sir, depends upon the sensitiveness of the chemical plate called his brain. There are brain-plates upon which everything impresses a permanent image; others, that catch only faint and feeble impressions; and still others,*" *that distort every object cast upon them. There are peo-ple, sir, who learn readily, people who learn little, and people who begin by knowing nothing, and go on accu-mulating ignorance to the end of their days."*

" WHAT ARE OPINIONS, AFTER ALL," muttered Mr. Bluff, *"but imperfect knowledge? We do not have opin-ions about the multiplication-table or the equinoxes. An opinion is simply an angle of reflection, or the facet which one's individuality presents to a subject, measuring not the whole nor many parts of it, but the dimensions of the reflecting surface. It is something, perhaps, if the reflection within its limits is a true one."*

CONTENTS.

BACHELOR BLUFF.

I.

INTRODUCING MR. BLUFF.

Mr. Oracle Bluff, who is commonly known among his friends and acquaintances as Bachelor Bluff, because of a disposition on his part to dwell upon his experiences as a bachelor, and among scoffers as Old Chatter Bluff, is a gentleman indisputably fond of talking, and very much inclined to believe that his opinions cover all the law and the facts. He is a gentleman whose years have reached sixty, whose figure is somewhat portly, who carries upon his shoulders a handsome, well-poised head, covered with scant silver locks. He has a broad brow, an ample, close-shaved chin, and a mouth which, though flexible, has as its general expression set lines indicative of a positive and downright character. His eyes are bright and restless, full of varying expression, sometimes flashing fire, and capable of sending furious glances

at opponents, or of bending upon presumptuous dis-
putants a look of overwhelming severity, and yet they
have been known upon occasions to melt into tenderness at some pathetic story.

Mr. Bluff has read a few books, glanced at a few
pictures, traveled a little, and seen something of
life; and, believing himself to have accumulated a
store of observation, is disposed to utter an opinion upon almost any subject that may be broached.
It must be conceded that these opinions are not
commonly borrowed, nor yet do they affect originality. They are usually the product of at least a
half-hour's meditation, it being Mr. Bluff's habit to
look penetratingly into any theme that comes before him, with the purpose of discovering its true
significance.

Mr. Bluff thinks himself wholly logical in all that
he says. He exhibits great confidence in his own
powers of penetration. He seems, indeed, to think
that it is his special mission to expose sophistries, put
shams to rout, and establish everything on a level
basis of sane reason. He is disposed to believe that
he possesses wide intellectual sympathies, and no
doubt indulgent listeners acknowledge the range of
his topics even if they sometimes question the fullness
of his intellectual comprehension. He prides himself
on his discernment and common-sense, but his com-

mon-sense is sometimes colored with a few tints of imagination. He is doubtless a little prone to Philistinism, the defect of nearly all robust thinkers, but he is not without sympathy for poetical and imaginative things. He is unfortunately a little deficient in humor—not that he can not enjoy a good joke, but he rarely ventures to perpetrate one. He does not usually see things on their comic side, and would be very likely to argue that the comic side of things is a distorted and falsified side, but he can distinguish the comic from the joyous and cheerful, and he often exhibits impatience at lachrymose views of life. Whatever else he may be he is at least honest, and frankly expresses just what he thinks, so that, whatever crotchets he may utter, they are heartily believed in by himself if by no one else.

Mr. Bluff's great fault is a determination always to do the greater part of the talking. He is the worst listener at his club, or in any circle where he chances to be; but fortunately his listeners are generally good-natured, and gracefully permit him to ramble on, contenting themselves with stimulating his utterances by throwing in remarks whenever there is indication that the conversation will flag. A very little mild contradiction, or an adroit suggestion, is all that is necessary to set the old gentleman off afresh on a new vein of argument and illustration; and when his listeners are tired of his discourse they quietly slip away, leaving him in possession of the field, even if not wholly victorious in the argument.

This is Bachelor Bluff. Talkative as he is, he is rather liked at his club; and it is to be hoped that his reputation will not suffer by an enlargement of his circle of listeners.

II

MR. BLUFF ON DOMESTIC BLISS.

(At Mr. Bluff's Bachelor Apartments.)

BACHELOR BLUFF,
Mr. CARRIWAY,
Mr. AUGER.

"As I am an old bachelor," exclaimed Bachelor Bluff, with an air as if he rather liked the imputation, "and generally esteemed a very crusty one, my ideas about domestic bliss are possibly considered of no moment. Not that I think so for my own part; indeed, I am convinced that the opinions I entertain on this subject are sound, dispassionate, and such as to commend them to all unprejudiced judges. I am aware, of course, that all old bachelors are supposed to see things with jaundiced eyes only; but the real truth is, they are unbiased 'lookers-on in Vienna,' see what others can not see, and penetrate through disguises by which others are deceived. And it has been so long the fashion to suppose that domestic bliss is something which bachelors neither understand nor appreciate—

a sort of sacred felicity that their obdurate hearts have not the virtue to embrace—that I am the more ready to utter my notions on the subject, just to show that, after all, the entrance into this charmed circle is not necessarily through the marriage-ring."

Bachelor Bluff paused, drummed for a few moments on his chair-arm, and then, finding that, while no one contradicted him, every one looked as if he were expected to go on, resumed:

"Now, a captious and unhandsome fellow might ask if there really is such a thing as domestic bliss, except in dreams. Are not the usual attempts to secure this social *ignis fatuus*, he would ask, marred by perversity of temper, opposition of ideas, and that general selfishness which the seclusion and *abandon* of home bring often so conspicuously to the surface? No doubt these questions would be pertinent in view of the kind of domestic bliss that commonly survives the arrangement known as matrimony; but the questioner would be inspired with another feeling were he to turn his regards upon that depreciated class known as old bachelors. As an illustration of the comparative felicities, in a domestic way, between the two conditions, let me draw a parallel, suggested by recent experience of my own—that is, if I shall not bore you."

"Go on! go on!" exclaimed all his listeners.

"It was only three weeks ago that I accepted an invitation to spend two days with my friend Appleby. Appleby is married. He has a wife—most married men have, you will say; but Appleby's wife makes him, as it were, many times married. Her presence, her individuality, her temper, her ideas, her wishes, her inches, surround and multiply upon him on all sides. Appleby has no room in his own house, and a very small corner in the outside world, so completely does Mrs. Appleby fill the boundaries of Mr. Appleby's sphere, and crush him into diminutiveness.

"I shall not soon forget the scene I beheld the first morning that I entered Appleby's breakfast-room. In the first place, it faced the north. This in itself is an evil. Then it was warmed economically by stray heat coaxed away from the kitchen-range below, and persuaded to diffuse itself within this circle of domestic bliss—which it ordinarily failed to do. This was simply an abomination. A breakfast-room not cheered in winter by a bright blaze is unworthy a place amid the domestic virtues. What more enlivening experience is there than that of coming down in the morning to a bright, cheery breakfast-room, in summer glad with the morning sun, in winter flushing and sparkling in the light of an open fire? But this deficiency was not all. Appleby's breakfast-room—it is a representative breakfast-room,

and for this reason I select it—was hung with var-
nished paper, and furnished with oak chairs and an
oaken buffet. Upon the walls were a few black, old-
fashioned prints, gloomy in wooden frames. The
floor was covered with an oak - colored carpet, because that cheerless color will not show crumbs.
The window-curtains were—but there were no window - curtains. The room was adorned in this particular with buff-tinted shades only. This was Appleby's breakfast-room, all garnished and beautified in
the fine spirit and under the perfect domination of
'domestic bliss.' And to this breakfast-room came
Mr. Appleby in slovenly dressing-gown and slovenly
slippers, Mrs. Appleby in an old shawl and curl-papers, and several young Applebys all in tumult and
snarling disorder. In this cheerless room, half-light-
ed, dull for want of cheerful tints in the furniture,
and for lack of a blaze on the hearth, arranged purposely for a hurried and comfortless matutinal meal,
the 'domestic bliss' of the Applebys showed itself in
a hundred irritabilities. And yet Appleby is always
boasting about his matrimonial felicities. He never
fails to introduce in our intercourse the subject of my
bachelor loneliness and discomfort, and honestly wonders why I do not set up in my bachelor quarters a
Mrs. Bluff (in curl-papers and faded silk, I suppose),
for the sake of companionship, and domestic comfort,

and all that. So much for a breakfast under the special dominion of feminine government.

Now, it was only three days after my breakfast with the Applebys, that I went to breakfast with genial John Bunker. Jack Bunker is a whole-souled fellow, who knows when a thing is *recherché*, and who has the wit to appreciate a bit of bachelor felicity. He always breakfasts in his library—this being the name his man James gives to his book-room—where he has a few books, a few pictures, and gathers all the little tasteful articles that he owns—a vase or two, a statuette, a rare print, a bit of china, all of which he tones up with warm upholstery. I, for my own part, like to eat in my best apartment; to partake of my meals under the pleasantest and most enlivening conditions. Eating and drinking is with me a fine art. That 'good digestion may wait on appetite and health on both,' I put my mind in its sweetest, its calmest, its most contented mood, by means of all the agreeable surroundings I can command. Hence I looked around Jack Bunker's cozy apartment, *tasting* all the points. There was a glowing blaze from bituminous coal in the low, polished grate. On a brass pendant stood the shining coffee-pot, from which issued low, murmuring music and delicious odors. The firelight was glancing up on the picture-frames, and the gilt backs of the books, on the warm-tinted walls

and the ceiling, and on drapery that fell over the
doorway, and partly shut out partly let in at the
windows the bright glances of light from the morning
sun.   Then the brilliant white cloth on the table, and
the easy-chairs for host and guest, and a new picture
only sent home the day before standing on an easel
near, and the morning paper warming by the fire—
well, it was a pleasant picture.   Jack rubbed his hands,
evidently enjoying the air of comfort, brightness, and
warmth, that filled the whole space, and delighted with
my appreciation of it all; and sat himself down in his
cozy chair, and invited me to mine, and looked around
at the books and the pictures, and hoped I was
pleased.

"I am not going to describe the breakfast further.
My sole purpose has been to draw two pictures, in
order to show that domestic bliss is not better understood or oftener realized by Benedicks than bachelors.
But no doubt some one will ask why all these conditions of domestic happiness are not possible with
'lovely women' to enhance the bliss of the scene."

"But think," said young Carriway, who had a
weakness for sentiment—" think of some beautiful
creature sitting by the side of the urn, serving your
coffee, applauding your pictures, listening to you as
you read a bit of news from the morning journal; perhaps, with her hands in yours, or with her dainty foot

on the fender, chatting with you softly but joyously over many pleasant themes."

"Humph!" replied Bluff, "it must be admitted that this is a pretty picture. But what if the 'lovely woman' comes down to the breakfast-room frouzy and fierce? What if she appears in a dressing-gown and curl-papers? What if she has a chronic fondness for *déshabillé?* What if she prove one of those whose nerves never get calm or in accord until after the morning is well passed? In my bachelor-home, domestic bliss is mine, beyond doubt; if I open the door to a 'lovely woman,' there is no telling what Pandora's box I shall uncover. Besides, it is a conviction of mine that refined and perfect domestic comfort is understood by men only."

"Heresy! heresy!" exclaimed half a dozen voices at once.

"Heresy it may be, but my opinion is well-grounded for all that. Women are not personally selfish enough to be fastidious in these things. They are usually neat to circumspection; but it is a cheerless and aggressive neatness—moral and inflammatory rather than luxurious and artistic. They are neat because they constitutionally hate dust, not because neatness is important to their own selfish comfort. Women are rarely epicureans. They have no keen enjoyment of eating and drinking, in dreams and laziness; they do not understand intellectual repose. It is not the quiet, the serenity, the atmosphere of home, that they at heart care about. Give a woman a new ribbon, and she will go without her dinner. Promise her a ball, and she will sit nightly for a month in a fireless room, muffled up in a shawl, and never murmur. She is fond of dress, not of comfort; of decoration, not of peace; of excitement, not felicity. And then, moreover, she is too willing to be ill-at-ease; too easily satisfied in all those things that pertain to personal comfort, and is far too much disposed to make the best of every thing, to enter fully into the necessity of creating domestic comfort. She likes home because there she has authority, there she receives her friends and shows her furniture, there she can give parties, and thereby get invitations to other parties. When matrimony introduces a man to *recherché* breakfasts, to perfect little dinners, to delightful social evenings, to perfectly-appointed parlors, then I shall believe that true domestic bliss is feminine in conception."

"To my mind," remarked Auger, a grave doctor of laws, "your notions about domestic bliss are dangerous and revolutionary. They will be construed into arguments against marriage; and marriage, you know, is the great conserver of public morality, and the great promoter of public welfare."

"But if I once succeed," retorted Bluff, "in

showing womankind that our domestic comfort is not, as society goes, a necessary consequence of marriage, the whole sex will set at work to make it so."

"No doubt," Auger replied, "if woman had reason to believe that she did not bestow this boon upon man, she would be sure to seek out the way to secure for him the felicity she knows so well how to appreciate for herself."

"Now, there you are wrong," exclaimed Bluff. "Women have no true appreciation of this domestic felicity, even while they have remained calm in the assurance that men, hungering for the peace of home, must come to them for it. They have, with very great egotism, scorned with a supreme scorn the idea of men being able to have anything orderly, neat, or tasteful, around them without women to supply the conditions. They have carried this idea so far as to look upon celibacy as not only a cheerless thing, but as by necessary implication a wicked thing; and yet instead of women being, as they suppose, the source of domestic bliss, they are radically and constitutionally its obstacles and enemies."

"There could be no home without women," exclaimed Carriway, with great warmth.

"I shall not quote history," replied the Bach-

elor, coolly, "to show that domesticity in women
has always been enforced; that in Eastern countries it is secured by compelled seclusion; that in
all times it has been the tyranny of man which has
subjected her to the boundary of home: but I will
simply give you a reason or two why in the nature
of things women have not the keen sympathy with
domestic felicity that men have—that is, if you care
to hear them."

"Go on."

"Men and women, as a consequence of their
distinct daily occupations, have very different aspirations and expectations in regard to matrimony.
How many of our young women, for instance, think
of domestic well-being as the desired end of marriage? Do they not contemplate the gayeties rather
than the serenities which marriage is to assure
them? Are not their marriage-dreams of balls, of
parties, of the opera, of visiting, of traveling? of
carriages, dresses, jewels, household splendor? of
social success, and the triumph of position at-
tained? Instead of Lares and Penates, do they
not dream of the dazzle and the dash of life?
And this is a natural consequence of their peculiar
position. Marriage is to give them their career,
and hence within it center all their ambitions, all
their hopes, all the largeness of their future. But,

with man, marriage is something very different. Men are out in the world, busy in the great battle of life — absorbed in its contests, filled sometimes with the triumph of success, and sometimes with the chagrin of defeat. Spurred by the stern necessity of achieving, they have surrendered all their energies to the struggle; they are busy with stratagems and manœuvres, keenly occupied with hopes and anxieties, and sometimes even struggling desperately against ruin. This is the life of the man; and this stirring career away from home renders home to him necessary as a place of repose, where he may take off his armor, relax his strained attention, and surrender himself to perfect rest.

"But home is not this to a woman. It is not her retreat, but her battle-ground. She does not fly to its shelter as an escape from defeat or for a temporary lull; it is her arena, her boundary, her sphere. To a woman the house is life militant; to a man it is life in repose. She at home is armed with all her energies; he at home has thrown down his arms. She has no other sphere for her activities: ordering her household, subduing its rebellions, directing its affairs, make up her existence. She bustles, she stirs, she controls, she directs, she exhausts herself in its demands, and then seeks for recreation and rest elsewhere. 'I am wearied,'

says the husband; 'let me sit by the fire and
smoke, and dream, and rest.' 'I am wearied,' says
the wife; 'let me be refreshed by a visit to my
friends, by an evening at the opera, at the theatre,
at the concert.'

"And so we see how a natural and radical an-
tagonism may exist between man and wife as to
the pleasures and the needs of home. Of course,
in a vast majority of cases, these antagonisms are
compromised. Between affectionate couples they
never break out into warfare; but they assuredly
exist, and two such distinct sets of ideas must be
watched by both husband and wife if they would
not have them the father of many discontents and
much infelicity. Do you not see how woman, by
the very necessities of her existence, must have a
different idea of home than what man has?"

"This," said Carriway, "is very like arguing
that the play of 'Hamlet' is better with the part
of Hamlet omitted. We all know the grace and
charm women give to life; we all think with pleasure of that spot which woman renders an oasis in
the desert of life."

"Yes, my dear sir, we all think of that oasis
because we love to contemplate it, because it is so
essential to our happiness. We make an ideal
home, and place an ideal woman in it; but, when

the reality comes, how confoundedly often we are disappointed ! "

" Do you then mean to say, flatly, that celibacy is better than marriage ? " asked Auger.

" By no means. What I hope to do is to convince ' lovely woman ' that, if we are to continue to marry her, she must endeavor to work up to our ideals of domestic felicity. She must try and find an outlet for her energies, so that at home she can fall into our luxuriousness, our love of repose, our enjoyment of supreme ease. You see women — I purposely do not use the word ladies — are very busy endeavoring to make a world of their ' pent-up Utica.' They sometimes are disposed to have it brilliant and animated ; but too often, in blind servility to one of their gods, Propriety, make it very cold and orderly. The amount of absolute cheerlessness a woman can stand is my amazement."

" Cheerlessness ! "

" Yes, cheerlessness," replied the Bachelor, emphatically. " Our women have an affection for flowers, ribbons, laces, silks, music, pets ; but are singularly insensible to cheerlessness. They like dark rooms. They prefer heat from a hole in the wall rather than from a bright blaze. They ask you to dine under a dim jet of gas. They will shiver through a cold storm in autumn, rather than

2

light a fire a day earlier than the almanac permits. A woman may have all the known virtues of her class ; all the gentleness, humility, grace, domestic virtue, poets have sung about — and yet, if you should ask for a blaze on the hearth on a dark, wet, chilly day in September, ten chances to one the request would be too much for her patience.

"Some women," continued the Bachelor, finding that no one interrupted him, "are slovenly—let us hope not many—I have seen untidy toilets, though ; but, when a woman is not slovenly, she is often so neat, trim, precise, methodical, and circumspect, that she excludes all color, all freedom, all *tone* from her house. Upon all forms of untidiness such a woman makes tempestuous warfare. Now, this is utterly destructive to domestic bliss—an essential element of which is ease and a sense of completeness. One can not be content if always under the smell of soapsuds, or if ceaselessly disturbed by the bustle of administration. The ultimatum of a woman's household luxury is apt to be the satisfaction of saying, 'There is not a speck of dust to be seen.' But this negative idea of home will not do. It is not sufficient to say there is no dust, no disorder, no untidiness, no confusion. We must have active ideas at work. We must have colors and sounds and sights to cheer, to refine, to delight us. But,

you see, to create a paradise of indolence, to fill
the mind with an ecstasy of repose, to render home
a heaven of the senses—women are usually too virtuous to do this. Daintiness in man takes an artistic form; in woman it assumes a formidable order, a fearful cleanliness, a precision of arrangement
that freeze us."

"But all this," broke in Carriway, "is no longer
the case. There was a time, no doubt, when your
picture would have been strictly true. But now
art has entered the house; color, banished by Pu-
ritan asceticism, has reasserted itself. Do we not
see on every hand the new arts and the new devices for making home beautiful?"

"For making home a museum!" growled the
Bachelor. "Yes, there is now a craze for what is
called household art, but it is for the most part
only a new form of cheerlessness, a passion for making the parlor a show-room, the splendor of which
must not be touched and scarcely looked upon save
by the outside world. It is art for Mrs. Grundy,
and not for the inmates of the house. Mrs. Grundy
is the power of powers. If a woman has only two
rooms in the world, one of these is furnished, garnished, set in order, and kept for the approbation
of that venerable lady. Domestic comfort must live
elsewhere than in the apartments devoted to this

lady—who exacts of all her devotees velvet carpet that must not be trod on, damask furniture that must not be sat on, and all forms of finery that must not be warmed by good, honest fires, lest the dust alight on them, or opened to the pleasant rays of the sun, lest his beams fade them. The disorder that sometimes is held up as domestic comfort I feel no sympathy with; domestic bliss is to my taste first-cousin to elegance, and an elegance that enters into one's daily being. Unless one is a man of wealth it is better to banish set-up conventional parlors altogether, and live and dine in the best apartment, seated among books, pictures, and the best furniture, invoke peace and comfort. Give us, I emphatically say, in our households color and cheeriness—not cold art nor cold pretensions of any kind, but warmth, brightness, animation. Bring in pleasing colors, choice pictures, *bric-à-brac*, and what-not; but let in also the sun; light the fires; and have everything for daily use."

"You have omitted one important thing," remarked Carriway.

"What is that?"

"Love!"

"Ah! that is something which bachelors, however agreeable they may make their apartments, must often sigh for. But love flourishes well when such notions as I have advanced are heeded; and then, men are such devotees of the senses, that so fair and delicate a thing as love will perish if women do not look well to make it a companion of domestic felicity."

"To my mind," said Auger, who had evidently been brooding intently over something, "we have driven out all the pleasure and sweetness of home in order to make room for a set of regulation comforts. We heat our houses by elaborate labor-saving furnaces; we light them with gas that flows into our rooms from far-off retorts; we have water, hot or cold, in our bedrooms at a touch; we surround ourselves with these numerous, well-ordered conveniences, and yet for every comfort we thus purchase we shut the door upon some felicity. The essential enjoyment of a pleasure, we must remember, is by contrast. We know what sunlight is by storm; what day is by night; what warmth is by cold; what the pleasures of the appetite are by hunger. The sweetness of labor past is often confessed; but we forget the sweetness of a comfort won. How can a family be cozy, confiding, cheerful, and united, around a blazing fire in the sitting-room, if every other apartment in the house is equally agreeable? When the temperature of a home in winter-time is the same throughout, the household hearth, so full of delightful associations, so honored in song and story, disappears. And, then, there is always a sacrifice of health in these uniformly-heated houses, especially with home-kept women. Used day after day to a uniform temperature, the moment they venture into the street the sharp change tells upon their sensitive flesh severely, and usually fastens a cold upon them. A pleasure is only enjoyed with thorough raciness and heartiness when it comes infrequently, or as a contrast: if we build ourselves up in organized ease, if we surround ourselves with methodized comforts, our 'primrose path of dalliance' may be easy to tread, but life will lose its keen relish, and satiety sooner or later extinguish our capacity for enjoyment."

There was a general murmur of assent to this, and then the conversation drifted to other themes.

III

MR. BLUFF'S THEORY OF POETRY.

(In the Library.)

A Poet,
Bachelor Bluff.

*Poet.** How is it that so many sensible people assume toward poetry an attitude of intellectual disdain ?

Bachelor Bluff. Perhaps because they *are* sensible people. The pretensions, the arrogance, the assumption of the poets, and the would-be poets, may well induce wise people to inquire what there is in this poetry which is so clamorously exalted.

Poet. I do not refer to people who find all poetry wholly without charm; these, unfortunately, are but too large in number. There are many persons who possess what usually passes for a decided poetic taste, who yet demand from the verses which they read little else besides a gratification of their rhyth-

* Much of what the Poet utters in this colloquy was contributed by Mr. Edgar Fawcett, but it appears here unedited by him.

mic sense on the one hand, and a general impression on the other that they are having things very pleasantly put. In not a few cases it would seem as if they looked upon poetry as a kind of mental retiring-room, where yawning, and stretching, and lolling upon cushions, must of necessity be admissible—as a place where one need no longer concern himself with the stricter exactitudes; where misrepresentation has an agreeable right to work its lawless will; where beauty is not solely its own excuse for being, but for being often rather scornful, as well, of how far reason restrains; and where grace, melody, and color, can form substitutes for solid thought no less efficient than attractive. I have frequently been struck with the way in which persons have welcomed certain ideas, when clothed poetically, which might have easily roused their worst polemic instincts if presented in a prosaic form. It is probable that this sudden toleration is less owing to the luxurious fascination of meter and rhythm than to a general understanding that matter has now become of slight importance, and manner delightfully the reverse. I confess that it amazes me to see a man of intellect holding passages of poetry in fond remembrance, which if written in prose he would never think of quoting; and I am now secretly of the belief that it is, after all, only "the mellow oes and aes" that he cares about, and that in his consideration the thought occupies something decidedly lower than a secondary place. The chief aim of all poetry is, no doubt, to be beautiful, but it is most loftily and enduringly beautiful when its thought is massive, profound, and original. Merely to expect from it soothative, agreeable, or sensuous effects, is to underrate its finest capabilities. Merely to seek emotional pleasure from it is to leave unemployed half its powers for giving pleasure at all.

Bluff. I do not agree with you; in fact, I affirm that the function of poetry is not *thought*, but *emotion*. The sole thing which distinguishes it from other forms of literary art is its metrical construction, in which lies the only power it possesses for giving pleasure which it does not share with all literature and the arts. It is really irritating to hear the claims put forth so continuously of the purposes, the functions, the attributes, the results, the what-not, of poetry, the majority of persons seeming to think that ideas, when expressed in accordance with certain metrical rules, attain an occult power which they could not possess in so-called plain prose. Now, these ideas do gain by the aid of rhythm a measurable force or power, but this is nothing more than the charm of melody — which

alone separates poetry from prose. The confusion
on this subject, however, is as extensive as human
nature. I doubt if accurate thinking or accurate
definition is possible. I am not thinking of the
dictionaries, but of efforts made by people generally
to indicate the essential quality or separate function
which anything possesses. I find, for instance, one
of our essayists affirming that the purpose and end
of poetry were never more accurately stated than in
the lines by Keats:

> " . . . It should be a friend
> To soothe the cares and lift the thoughts of man."

I advise you to quote those lines to any person not
acquainted with them, and ask him to guess what
it is that is to act as this " friend." Can that be
called a definition or description of anything which
applies with equal pertinency and force to a hundred other things? The lines by Keats are just as
true of music, of painting, of eloquence, of imaginative prose, as they are of poetry, and they really
apply with greater truth to religion than to anything
else. If we want to know the true value, the real
purpose, the exact quality of anything, we must discover what it possesses that separates it from other
things — what faculty, or function, or principle, or
law, pertains to it alone, and by which it may be

distinguished. Now, why is there poetry? What is its excuse for being? What distinctive quality does it possess? What special end has it in view? What are the features or signs by which it may be known?

Poet. Poetry, like wit, humor, and even art, can not be accurately defined. Its essence is subtile, its qualities illusive, and, although there are poets who divine its secret, no one has been able to put his divination into the form of a definition.

Bluff. No one, I grant, has been able to define or explain the secret of the charm which melody exerts upon us; and neither can the charm of color or form be explained; but the definition of poetry is simply that it is a form of literary expression which employs meter — a metrical arrangement of syllables with the purpose of delighting the ear by rhythmic beat and recurrence of sound. It is the stem from which music has separated into a special development.

Poet. This is nothing more than a definition of verse. You limit your terms wholly to the mechanical execution of lines—to that feature which addresses the ear, ignoring altogether the essence and true spirit of poetry—its embodiment of the beautiful, its exaltation, its inspiration and insight, its crystallization of thought, its power of picture-making, its profound moods and divinations. It is monstrous to assume that poetry is merely a succession of words in a smooth and sensuous order. So far from this being true, I affirm that it primarily incarnates the beautiful, but achieves its highest function only when it is philosophical and profound. Buckle goes so far as to say that the abstract methods of poetry act as stimuli to precise scientific investigation, that it is often the *avant-courrier* of detailed and formulated knowledge, throwing its light over lands into which science has not yet ventured. "There is in poetry," he says, "a divine and prophetic power which, if properly used, would make it the ally of science instead of the enemy. By the poet, Nature is contemplated on the side of the emotions; by the man of science, on the side of the understanding. But the emotions are as much a part of us as the understanding. They are as truthful; they are as likely to be right. Though their view is different, it is not capricious. They obey fixed laws; they follow an orderly and uniform course; they run in sequences; they have their logic and method of inference. Poetry, therefore, is a part of philosophy, simply because the emotions are a part of the mind. If the man of science despises their teaching, so much the worse for him. He has only half his weapons; his arsenal is unfilled." This places poetry, you see, side by side with the highest intellectual efforts; it establishes that its mission is not merely to be musical, not solely to be sensuous, not exclusively to be beautiful, but to go hand-in-hand with the intellect in its profoundest philosophical pursuits and studies.

Bluff. My good sir, the works of the great poets exhibit all the transcendent qualities you have enumerated—beauty, wisdom, inspiration, insight, divination, exaltation, philosophy—all are there; but beauty, wisdom, divination, philosophy, are all found just as strikingly in the great prose-writers as in the poets. There is not one thing, not one, which you have set down as the attribute of poetry that exclusively belongs to it. All that Buckle says pertains to imagination and the emotions; he is using the word poetry in the popular sense, as if it were synonymous with beauty and certain exalted mental qualities. He simply affirms the value of the imagination as compared with reason, and exalts the emotions as forces even in purely intellectual pursuits ; and surely imagination and emotion are as competent to act as handmaids to science and philosophy in elevated prose as in poetry. Prose is capable of expressing the whole range of human thought, human aspiration, human feeling; of reaching the heart, of rousing the imagination, of stirring

the emotions, of exciting the fancy ; it possesses
every weapon and every resource the poet is endowed with, excepting the single one of melody.
Come, here is a volume of Tennyson at my hand.
Let me open it at random, and read the first passage that falls under my eye. . . . . I have hit upon
" The Princess," and here are a few lines that my
eye alights upon :

> " . . . Out we paced,
> " I first, and, following through the porch that sang
> All round with laurel, issued in a court
> Compact of lucid marbles, bossed with lengths
> Of classic frieze, with ample awnings gay
> Betwixt the pillars, and with great urns of flowers.
> The Muses and the Graces, grouped in threes,
> Enringed a billowing fountain in the midst ;
> And here and there on lattice edges lay
> Or book or lute."

This is a captivating picture; it is a perfect piece
of word-painting: but how easy to transpose it all
into prose, losing thereby just the ineffable charm
of metrical arrangement — *just this and no more !*
Study it well, and you will see there is no known
means by which it can be distinguished from prose
excepting its meter—and this, consequently, makes
it poetry.

Poet. Carry this out, and any piece of doggerel

is poetry, no matter how empty, vacant, worthless, it may be.

Bluff. Just as a poor picture in color must be classed, like Titian's " Venus " or Murillo's " Assumption," as painting; just as the naturalist under the term mammalia must group the mouse and the lion. Classification in these things is not by *quality*, but by *structure ;* by the latter we have the *kind*, by the former the *rank*.

Poet. The mere use of rhythm does not of itself separate the two forms. If we say, " The moon arose," we have measure and rhythm, but assuredly not poetry ; if we say, " The moon unveiled her peerless light and threw across the scene her silver mantle," we have the fact expressed in poetry—and it would still be poetry if we reconstructed the sentence so as to exclude the meter.

Bluff. This is the difference between the *simple* and the *ornate*, and not the difference between prose and poetry. If it were so, nineteen twentieths of our poetry would have to be remanded to prose— including nearly all that Wordsworth and his followers have written. Twist the theory as you will, you will find that meter is the quality, and the only quality, that indicates poetical composition. If there is anything else in poetry which prose does not possess, point it out.

Poet. Poetry crystallizes ideas, concentrates a world into a phrase, expounds a philosophy in a sentence. It is sinewy with thought, it is a succession of captivating pictures, it ennobles and transfigures, it glorifies with splendid colors, it reveals with searching analysis, it embodies the highest wisdom, gives form to the most glorious dreams, fixes and shapes a thousand otherwise illusive beauties. Rhythmical utterance is its vehicle only. The quality which makes metrical lines poetry is something that utterly escapes analysis; and in this discussion it is well to keep in mind the original meaning of the word—which is, to *make*, to *create*. The poet, when fulfilling his true office, is a creator, a seer.

Bluff. It is this original significance of the word which has led to all the ecstatic utterances on the subject. The poet preceded the prose-writer; his songs and hymns were the sole vehicle for the expression of imaginative ideas, for the relation of heroic deeds, for the utterance of emotional thought. Poetry was the whole of literature. The poet was a maker and seer not because he sung in numbers, but because he was the voice of prophecy, the chronicler of history, the teacher of morals, the expositor of the passions and the sentiments. To-day literature and the arts in their various forms do now for mankind what the poet did in the beginning of civilization. In some things prose accomplishes this end better than poetry. You say, for instance, that poetry crystallizes ideas. Now, the very best crystallized thought is in our proverbs, which for the most part are in prose. It happens sometimes that the requirements of rhythm or rhyme lead to great compactness, but it also sometimes happens that they lead to padding and feeble extension. Neither compactness nor verbiage is, therefore, an inevitable or necessary condition of poetry — the arbitrary long and short syllables and terminal rhymes determining absolutely which of these two things shall characterize a line. Crystallization, moreover, implies accuracy of thought and clearness of thought. In neither of these things has poetry any advantage over prose. In prose we can choose with utmost precision the exact word or phrase we need ; in poetry the recurring beat is tyrannical, and is just as likely to enforce an obscure as a luminous phrase. The rhyme and the meter often lead to awkward inversions and forced expressions that are fatal to clearness and precision of thought. All that the poetical form can do is to help fix an idea in the memory by a sonorous ring, or by smooth and flowing cadence. Coleridge has defined poetry as the best word in the best place. This is not a definition of poetry, but a definition of *style*. The poet selects the best word he can, but is often compelled to surrender the most accurate word for one that will better meet the requirements of his versification—to which, as Byron tells us, all things must yield.

Poet. This I grant; but the other high qualities that I have named, they assuredly are not so much a·function of prose as of poetry.

Bluff. They may not be as commonly found in prose as in poetry, but prose can reach any height of imagination or expression that poetry can. Witness the great orations. Would one of Burke's splendid speeches be fuller of strong thought, of more brilliant fancies, of more swelling diction, of more inspired fervor, of greater imaginative reach, had it been thrown into verse—had it supplemented these things with the best resources of the poets? Cast one of his orations into poetry, and it would lose in clearness, directness, and force; but there would be passages the beauty of which would be greatly enhanced by meter and cadence, and certain lines would ring in the ear with a resonance never to be forgotten.

Poet. But there are subtiler melodies in poetry than the melody of numbers. In true poetry words are wedded by affinities too delicate to be formulated into rules. Every one knows the laws for constructing blank verse, but how few can write really good lines of this character!

Bluff. Every one knows the rules of composition, but how few can write good prose! There are as many harmonies and subtilties in prose as in poetry—the arrangement of words by nice and perfect fitness is as possible and almost as difficult in one form as in another.

Poet. But poetry is always necessarily identified with fancy and imagination; we exact of it those conditions, and can think of no excuse for its being unless it carries the mind into realms of beauty.

Bluff. There is no excuse for any art unless it does just this thing—unless it stirs the emotions and exalts the imagination. This is the special domain of all art. We are charmed with the ideas, the pictures, the imagery, the fancies, the conceits, the suggestions, the beauty, so generally found in poetry, and thus are seduced into the idea that these things *make* poetry, forgetting that they exist in entire independence of special modes of expression. Now, that which constitutes a painting is *color ;* it is not the story, the ideas, the hundred other things that please us therein : everything else but color may be expressed by literature, or sculpture, or drawing in black-and-white. A painting *is* a painting by the employment of pigments, and worthily so by rightly using them. Sculpture separates itself from other forms of art by the fact of its being form in relief; whatever other charm or quality it possesses does not belong to it *because* it is sculpture. It is barren enough if beauty and imagination are not in it, but, while these things may determine the *rank* of a work by the chisel, they do not determine its classification. It is therefore a particular method that makes poetry, not the ideas that leaven the performance, that elevate it, that consecrate it, that make it glorious. These are the qualities that make verse *great* poetry.

Poet. Every mind is fixed in the idea that poetry means beautiful thought, and not the sing-song of the meter. We often hear a beautiful sunset described as poetical. A charming fancy is always crowned as poetical.

Bluff. It would be just as logical to characterize a beautiful sunset or a fine conceit as sculpturesque! We can not get accurate understanding on this subject by calling in popular confusion as a witness. We may sweep all the poetical literature in the world out of existence, let the art of versification perish, and yet we would not abridge in the least the dreams, the fancies, the conceits, or any of the emotional or imaginative forces of the world.

Poet. It is not worth while uttering the truism

that emotion and imagination exist without poetry. No one will deny it. But the poet appropriates and exalts them; he gives them habitation, form, and expression; he unites them with all other attributes of the mind. The supreme quality of poetry, its exalted service, is not that it charms the ear, or pleases the fancy, or interests the intelligence, but that it *simultaneously* appeals to the several sides of our nature involved in the mind, the emotions, and the senses. It is the *consensus* of several things that makes poetry. Its dominion is over the whole being. It reasons, it thinks, it feels, it dreams; while its cadence charms the ear, and its warm pictures lull the senses, its outflying thoughts compass the world.

Bluff. This simultaneous action upon the intellect and the senses, this *consensus* of many qualities which make poetry worthy, is necessary to give *any* human work of the imagination a high place. As to thinking, that has little place in poetry or in any art. Poets dream and make pictures—this is about all. The notion which you seemed to find sanctioned in Buckle, that the mere metrical arrangement of words can aid in thinking, promote good thinking, or be anything else than an incumbrance to accurate thinking, is absurd. Poetry has an abundance of enthusiasm, passion, emotion, idealization, sensuous charm, but little or no real thought. Those who are to do genuine thinking must clear themselves of every possible obstruction—all rules of form, all dictations of method, all devices that allure the senses.

Poet. Enthusiasm and passion are only the garment clothing the clear and definite idea within. You must recollect that, to have the mirage, we must have the actuality. The mountain is still a mountain, whether we see it in its rugged lines, or when it looms a changing mass of violet vapor. John Stuart Mill has written on the woman's-rights question, and Tennyson has also written upon it in "The Princess." In the prose of one writer there is the able discussion of a subtile question, after a manner no less powerful than limpid, and marked by particularizations, items, specializations. In the verse of the other writer there are supreme fervor, a splendid picturesqueness, and every possible accessory of fine rhythm and mellow voweling. One is deliberative and practical thought, the other emotional and desultory. One is a landscape whose least grass-blade, bough, or road-line, meets us with vivid distinctness; the other is the same landscape flooded with transfiguring moonlight, its most salient features alone visible, and these softened or made sublime.

Bluff. This is the difference between exact logic and the suggestiveness, the breadth, the half-touches of *art*. All that poetry does is to heighten these art-effects by the mysterious charm of cadence—for cadence in its effect upon the human mind may be fairly called mysterious. We know that color simply as color is a great delight; while the fine proportions and graceful lines of form have the capacity to thrill and fascinate us. In the same way mere mellow syllables have the power to create sweet sensations. If these musical syllables are nothing but empty sound, why not write in prose? You have heard the winds moan and whisper in the tree-tops; you have listened to the fall of water over rocks, and the splash of fountains; you know the charm of a soft voice in woman : these are evidence of what a quality in Nature mere sound is. Now, I make the bold assertion that poetry exists solely because of the delight of the human ear in cadence and mellow sound.

Poet. Why, then one needs only neat blendings of vowels and consonants for the making of poetry.

Bluff. If the cadence were united to purely empty and meaningless words, all our other senses would revolt against the lines. But the charm of cadence is so great that it seems to clothe vagueness and obscurity with meaning, and will seduce a

reader into admiring lines that he can not define
or explain, the meaning of which but faintly glim-
mers in his mind. I have often been struck, when
hearing poets read their verses, how completely the
musical idea predominated. It is said that Tennyson reads his own poems in a monotonous sing-
song. Within my experience, I have never heard a
poet recite poetry in a manner to show that he had
the least idea of its meaning; he invariably thinks
of nothing but the cadence. If there were no
meaning, then the verses, of course, would excite
disdain. But in many cases any form of half-hinted
suggestion suffices—and vagueness, let me say, is legitimately a force and quality in poetry, just as it is
in all art. It is found in the greatest poets, as in
the greatest artists, and completely establishes the
axiom that poetry is not thought, but feeling. It is
related that in Turner's time a well-known engraver
called upon the great artist for an explanation as to
the meaning of a vague shape in one corner of a
painting which he had undertaken to reproduce on
steel. "What do you think it is?" gruffly asked
the painter. The engraver hesitatingly replied that
he didn't know, but perhaps it was a wheelbarrow.
"Well, make it a wheelbarrow," exclaimed the
painter, and turned on his heel. The painter had
in his mind a scheme of color, and was wholly in-

different to details of form. In the same way a poet often makes and masses impression by felicitous sound, in which there is but uncertain and illusive sense.

Poet. I must admit that much of our modern poetry has the sins of obscurity and wordiness. The first, as in the case of Browning, often conceals much sinewy and laudable thought; the second but too often conceals a disheartening vacuum. There are songs scattered through Swinburne's poem, " The Sailing of the Swallow," which are simply a collection of gaudy-colored words, that may mean almost anything one pleases to have them mean. They are the hollow shell of poetry—rainbow-tinted, it is true, but without any æsthetic right to exist. It is in the most perfect blending of the sweetest sound with the noblest sense that poetry finds her loftiest and best expression. When the first preponderates over the second (as it is constantly doing in Browning's work), the result is crude, inharmonious, and often even repulsive. When (as we too often find in the case of Swinburne) there is a great deal of rhythm and color, and very little else besides, the artistic error is still more grave. I do not mean that this perfect union is always to be sought for, but I maintain that even in the simplest ballad a certain dignity of idea is

3

indispensable. Among poems which are passionate expressions of sorrow, longing, despair, or religious faith, the higher imaginative traits are out of place; but here, as always, no amount of rhetorical elegance may properly hide an underlying platitude. Yet, in all the more ambitious conceptions, this stately equipoise is to be aimed for. Milton accomplished it in his epic, or at least grandly approximated toward its accomplishment. Pollok, in his, fell short on the intellectual and not the metrical side. In Pope the two elements of the combination were excellently suited one to another, though neither was of the lordlier ideal sort. Keats erred extravagantly in the direction of voluptuous phrasing, often almost smothering his thoughts in mere mode of utterance, or making them pass before the reader like shapes that staggered beneath burdens of flowers. Shelley came very near, in certain instances, wedding "perfect music unto noble words"; and perhaps no writer of any time has acquired a more superb evenness between the thing said and the manner of saying it than Tennyson. We have all heard of "the light that never was on sea or land." It is precisely this light which, if thrown over certain objects, must produce in all cases the exquisite and unexplainable effect called "poetry." But if the object does not exist—if the light be thrown upon vacuity—what wonder if the result has still a beauty which in not a few cases annoys us by the meaningless charm which it exerts?

Bluff. "The light that never was on sea or land," let me tell you, is simply the light bestowed by imagination; it glows in Turner's skies, in the eloquence of Burke, in the prose of Ruskin; it is shared by the poets with all others who are touched with the fire of inspiration.

IV

MR. BLUFF'S IDEAL OF A HOUSE.

(*At the Club.*)

BACHELOR BLUFF,
A DREAMER.

" I PICTURED to myself, the other day, in a half-dream," said the Dreamer, " a house which embodied all the latest and best ideas of taste and art-culture."

" It must have been a dream, indeed ! " exclaimed Bachelor Bluff, turning restlessly in his chair. "But, pray, what did your sleeping imagination set forth as the ideal of a house ? "

" It was a house like a symphony—all in harmony, and tone, and perfect keeping. Color was the silent music of this house ; form and proportion were the foundations of its being. It was a house in which there were beauty, repose, peace, and sweetness. The eye rested with lasting pleasure upon fine adjustments of beautiful objects, and the mind found intellectual stimulus in treasures of painting, marble, and bronze."

"Yes, I see! Your dream was of a house toned up, so to speak, to a high-art pitch—one of Whistler's 'symphonies of color.' Well, this is not new in the world of dreams. I am not sure but it would be as well if houses of the kind existed only as a fantastic nothing of the imagination. There was a time when the ideal of a perfect house was one which bloomed with thriving olive-branches—a nest where under protecting wings life came into being, expanded, filled all the spaces with love and music, and which eventually sent out into the world hearty and honest souls fit to cope with it and to adorn it. But now the ideal house is a *bric-à-brac* shop. Nevertheless, let me hear further."

"In the house I imagined," continued the Dreamer, "there entered the matured and perfect knowledge of a trained taste—there were no incongruities, no vulgarities, no discords. It exhibited in its plan both a severe and a liberal mind; it had harmony and unity with abundant variety. Just as we find in Nature rich contrasts, manifold details, and broad effects and masses, so the appointments and adornments of this house were blended into a consistent and delightful whole."

"This is all very well for generalization," said the Bachelor. "But my imagination can not live on mere summaries. I wait for some of the details in the furnishing of this marvelous mansion."

"Our dreams are apt, you know, to grasp at a detail here and there, but they rest content in the main with vague, half-defined pictures; but I will recall all the particulars I can of my Utopian house. The first thought, apparently, of the artistic decorator in regard to each room was to inquire whether it was to be beautiful in itself, or a place into which beautiful things were to be gathered. If the latter, then the walls, ceiling, floors, were considered simply as foils for the articles and objects which were to be set off against them. Imagine a drawing-room the walls of which were covered with a paper of warm olive tint, through which intertwine with glints of gilt a slightly-defined leaf-pattern—a mere suggestion of form, just sufficient to break the monotony of the tint. The result was walls which, while in themselves a charm to the eye, were nevertheless but little more than a background against which form and color had pure and perfect relief. In the dado below were definite forms and colors, though still subdued, while the frieze beneath the cornice was of rich Pompeian device and color. It is needless to say that this principle of wall-decora-

tion now enters many houses, but it is still wholly
unknown to innumerable people, who seem unconscious that markings, devices, and figures on the
wall mix with and confuse the figures and colors
that adorn the objects placed against it. Color
against color, paintings against painting, we still see
in many houses. And yet no flat, whitened surface,
no raw, cold tint, even if without pattern or devices, can serve as a suitable background for paintings or prints. No ingenuity in the multiplication
of pictures, or in the adjustment of furniture, can
make a room of this kind anything but raw and
discordant. In this parlor of my imagination there
were hung against the satisfying negative of the
walls a few paintings of captivating beauty, all
framed in such a way that the frames, instead of
competing with the pictures, as is so often the case,
humbly served to heighten their effect. These paintings were not tragedies, nor histories, nor portraits,
nor narratives. They had no stories to tell but the
story of beauty. There were no groups of men and
women busy at nothing, and projecting noisy costumes upon the scene. The pictures, for the most
part, were landscapes full of poetry and tenderness;
they were delicious moods of Nature, studies munificent in color, and rich with mellow depths of mysterious shadows. Who looked upon these paintings

slipped away into dreams; he was transported to Elysium; there stole over him rest, and peace, and contentment."

"I certainly shall not quarrel with your ideas of pictures. How about the furniture of this wonderful room?"

"I declare I do not know whether the furniture was Gothic or Renaissance, Queen Anne, or buhl. I think there was no exactness of style; I remember only that each object seemed in itself beautiful, and rightly adjusted to the beauty and character of every other object. The divans, sofas, chairs, all exhibited repose and simplicity, with great purity of form and suitable variety of line, with but little carving, and this a part of the wood, instead of an adjunct to it. They were covered with stuffs the texture and tints of which resembled Eastern rugs; they were soft, so as to suggest ease and repose to the body, and of colors whose subdued blendings gave ease and repose to the eye. There were no doors, the bald and ugly panels of which no art can redeem; but instead curtains draped the entrance-ways, hung from ebony poles. There were hanging cabinets, also of ebony, but picked out with tiles and ornaments, which were filled with specimens of porcelain that were valuable because rare, but more valuable because selected with admirable perception of harmony of color and elegance of form. There were shelves with artistic bronzes, medallions, and gems; and an easel which held rare etchings. All about, indeed, were objects of great beauty; the eye and the mind felt both stimulated and rested by a variety that was not confusion, by a splendor that in its several parts was harmonious and admirable. I have neglected to say that the carpet, which covered only the middle space of the room, resembled the walls in not being decorative in itself, but the base for decorative objects to stand upon. The pile was thick, the texture soft; figures it had none, its color being a warm gray with a red gleam in it; there were upon it two or three rugs of rich dyes, which relieved what might otherwise have been a monotony of tone; and the easel, the ample chairs, the cabinets, the screens, the divans, all stood painted, as it were, against this modest foil. The windows were studies. The curtains could at a touch be so swept aside as to let in the full splendor of the sun, or closed to shut it wholly out when desirable. But why descant upon these details, when not details but the rich oneness, the unity, the perfect *ensemble*, constituted its supreme charm, its artistic claims? Other rooms—"

"Oh, describe no more!" interrupted Bluff, impatiently. "An upholsterer would do it better. All that can be said of your ideal house is that it is a museum, the different objects of which have been selected with care and an artistic perception of their relations to each other. At heart you are like the rest of the world just now — in love with toys, household confusion, and show. The other day I nearly broke my neck over Mrs. Clutter's tiger-rug. Why are there tiger-rugs, I demand to know? Why must people, in blind subjection to the tyrant Fashion, make their houses preposterous curiosity-shops? Mrs. Clutter's house, and not your ideal, is the true example of the prevailing rage. She has shut out all the light from her windows with horse-hair curtains an inch thick, which once would not have been thought good enough for horse-blankets. She has laid down her floors in many-colored rugs so thickly that one might think himself in a carpet-dealer's ware-rooms; and the visitor must be wary or he'll be tripped up by them at every step. She has covered her walls with gorgeous jugs, bowls, jars, urns, vases, of every conceivable variety, in which for the most part ingenuity in the way of ugly design has done its worst. She has hung screens in her doorways, and cabinets over her mantels. She has mounted old brass fire-dogs over her book-shelves, and planted emblazoned shields

of metal over her door-lintels. She has bought all
the old worm-eaten furniture she could find, and
asks you to sit on chairs that were made for mankind before backbones were discovered. She has
turned the gas out of the house, and illuminated it
with painted candles. She goes to bed with a
Roman candlestick, sleeps under a Moorish rug,
eats off of cracked china discovered in a Marble-
head fisherman's cottage, wears a mediæval gown
that is all straight lines; and she talks all day of
Medicean porcelain, of Roman *amphoræ*, and Etruscan vases; of *grès de Flandre*, Dutch delft, and
Raffaellesque and mezza-majolica; of Palissy and
Henri Deux, of Chinese celestial blue and crackle,
of Japanese *cloisonné*, old Satsuma, and Hispano-Mo-
resque, of Sèvres and *pâte-sur-pâte*, of Chippendale
and Eastlake furniture, of Queen Anne and Renaissance and Marie Antoinette, and so on *ad infi-
nitum*, with a skill at quoting catalogues and running off names that is amazing. Is this a true
house that is made up of curious trifles from the
shops — that is simply a chaos of colors, knick-
knacks, and all forms of fantastic foolishness? Are
there breadth, humanity, heart, life, dignity, intellect,
felicity, in this jumble of misnamed art? Unless
art broadens the imagination and stirs the faculties,
there is no excuse for its being; but the art that

Mrs. Clutter is prostrate before dwarfs the imagination, narrows the intellect, and impoverishes the whole nature. She has no sympathy with men and women; it is all absorbed by her teacups and saucers. She has no perceptions of life except as a surrender of the mind to her paltry toys, and she is more concerned in the downfall of a cracked plate than in the wars and calamities that afflict the world outside of her bazaar. Her children are hidden away in nurseries; she dares not permit them to bring their active bodies and restless spirits into her rooms, lest they knock down her glass screens or break her precious jars. Emphatically, Mrs. Clutter's variety-shop is not a home. Now, as you have set forth your dream of an ideal house, let me picture mine.

"Your ideal is a town-house: let me go into the country for mine. The house that comes up in my imagination has breadth, largeness, and simplicity. It is honest, serene, and hospitable. It is not a castor-box with many towers and turrets and roofs; it is not a jumble of ill-contrived rooms; it is not a pagoda, nor an ornamental *chalet*, nor an Italian villa. It is not a dry-goods box crushed under the weight of a Mansard-roof, like a small boy under his grandfather's hat. There are no fancies, nor fantastic devices, nor contortions, nor cheap attempts at loud decoration, in the house that I see in my mind's eye. It has no cupola, real or make-believe; but it has two or three genuine balconies, and it is without even that universal favorite in our country, a gallery commonly (but erroneously) called a piazza."

" I am glad in all your negatives to catch at one affirmative—there are balconies, which fact is a beginning, at least, of this shadowy nondescript. But why, in the name of summer comfort, do you abolish the veranda—or piazza, according to common parlance ? "

" Because the sun and the light and the air must enter with ease and breadth into the house I imagine—and covet. An ample porch gives every facility for summer *al fresco* sitting and reading that a veranda does. The house of my fancy sits low. Its wide door is approached by a broad and deep covered porch, whose paved foundation lifts but a few inches above the grass that encompasses it on its three open sides. The windows each side of the porch are also wide and low, with eglantine and honeysuckle twining around them. These flow-ering vines keep out neither air nor light, but send into the recesses of the rooms a summer fragrance that is always delicious and refreshing. They are better studies in colors than painted tiles ; they are

more radiant in beauty than *cloisonné* or majolica;
they give to the interior a charm which Mrs. Clutter's most desperate efforts can not even hint at;
their freshness, sweetness, and beauty, fill all the
space with fascination. Your veranda-inclosed house
banishes this *bric-à-brac* of Nature to a distance. In
my ideal house sweet blossoms must grow at its
feet, they must twine lovingly about its windows,
their odors must enter its rooms, and their freshness give perennial charm to the life within. I do
not imagine many details in the exterior of the
house. There are balconies, as I have said, that
are not make-believe adjuncts, but ample and ser-
viceable structures, which permit me and mine to
sit within them under the open sky, shadowed only
by the branches of the trees that stand all around
the house. I see also pointed gables, and chimneys
of carved brick after the old, quaint, Tudor fashion.
The house is not of wood, that at one time dazzles
with the glare of new paint, and at another is
ragged and out-at-elbows, as it were, with weather-
stains and dilapidation. It is of stone that softens
and grows mellow with the passing years, that gathers tone, and not stains, from the rain and the sunshine, and which permits the vines to cling to it
without getting rotten and sodden under them.
Can we ever have houses that will fill us with a

sense of their strength and perpetuity, as if their foundations were deep, their walls a protection, their roof an ægis, if we continue to build our frail structures of clapboards?

"But let me change the scene. I can not re-lease you until you have seen my ideal house—a plain, practical sort of ideal so far, as you concede —in its winter interior."

"I do not see that your house differs essentially from many mansions in England."

"Where, among countless ugly structures, are many that are admirable ideals of the rural house. If we ingraft some of the best features of English picturesque cottages upon the best features of their manors, with a hint or two borrowed from our own architecture, we shall have a country-house that is ideal only because it does not exist, it being quite as easy of accomplishment as are the strange mon-sters that spring up in the suburbs of every town in the country.

"But let me take you into my winter-rooms, as I picture them. In that season we have the liveliest sense of the beneficence, serenity, and comfort, of home. And here let me paint my scene by freely using negatives and contrasts. Those suburban mon-strosities of which I have spoken keep out the wind and the rain, and here ends pretty much every real

service they render. They have no felicities. The
floors are covered usually with glaring carpets; the
chilling white walls of the rooms are ornamented
with dreary, black engravings, or with hideous
chromos. The fireplace is banished, and the sole
warmth is from the sickening stove or the more
sickening furnace. There are often books to read,
for Americans have intellectual capacity even with
low artistic perceptions. Newspapers and magazines, at least, abound; and there is inevitably a
piano. But the scene is chilling and dreary. There
is no feeling of repose or ease; nothing to charm
the senses into restfulness. This is too often the
picture of our suburban, and sometimes of our ur-
ban, interiors.

"I have a dream of another scene. The snow
whirls and scurries without; the trees sway and
groan in the wind; the sky and land are darkening
as the shadows of night come apace—so let us enter. Ah, here is compensation! There is blaze,
there is warmth, there is light, there is an over-
flowing of strange beauty. The walls, you quickly
see, are not of chilling plaster that peels and chips
off; nor of paint that is always hard and artistically
unmanageable; nor of paper that stains so readily,
and which ever obtrudes its senseless patterns.
They are wainscoted to the cornice with wood

crossed by a dado-rail, and ornamented with a few incised carvings. The wood is shellacked or stained of a reddish tint, which catches and reflects the light from candles or fire-blaze with rich effect. A vast chimney, which is a fine piece of architectural projection, has an open fireplace, in which logs are blazing. The mantel is heavy, and holds spreading candelabra, and a vase or two. Even a little *bric-à-brac* enters my country-house—but very little, be certain. Upon the walls hang several pictures of superb color — rich, still-life subjects that glow in deep tones, and catch radiant lights from the blaze on the hearth. Still-life subjects are chosen because this room with its dark walls might be somber were there not marked foci of color. But it is not somber. The floor, as I see it, is warm with a central carpet of rich dyes. There are large tables, massive and commodious chairs, many books — books are, indeed, abundant; they lie on the tables, and fill low shelves that skirt two sides of the room. Warm-colored stuffs hang over the windows to exclude intruding draughts of air, and doors open into an adjoining room similarly furnished, save that a hospitable sideboard looks festive with china and glass.

"Mark what it is that I see in my vision—a room of space, color, light, and tone; where there

is neither emptiness nor profusion, neither glitter nor
dreariness; where there are breadth and substance,
charm for the eye, restfulness for the soul, animation for the spirit.

"And, after all, what is any picture unless human
life comes in to grace it? I see in my dream fair
girls on summer days sitting in the framework of
my vine-trellised windows; I watch in my winter
vision young women in soft, graceful drapery mov-
ing resplendent in the glow of the fire-light; I hear
merry voices, and see bright faces, and catch the
gleam of tender eyes; and over all broods the
spirit of harmony and peace. This is my ideal.
Art is there, but it is a handmaid, not a tyrannical
fashion. There are correctness without severity, simplicity without baldness, decoration without fussi-
ness, beauty without frivolity, and every place is for
occupancy, and everything for use. We eat under similar pleasant conditions; our chambers have
warm hangings, cheerful blaze on their hearths,
good pictures on their walls. Handsome boys and
fair girls give felicity to this house, and they borrow from it their profoundest peace. Let each
man put into his dream the house that he loves—
I have given you with off-hand touches the ideal
of mine."

The Bachelor paused. Was that a mist that

dimmed his eyes? Who shall say what memories of "handsome boys and fair girls" once alive in his fancy, but which a perverse fate had rendered impossible, were now bringing that dew to his eye-lids?

V

MR. BLUFF ON FEMININE TACT AND INTUITIONS.

(In the Drawing-Room.)

MIRANDA,
BACHELOR BLUFF.

"You must admit, Mr. Bluff," remarked Miranda, in her smoothest and most persuasive tones, "that women are superior to men in their intuitions."

"Admit it!" exclaimed Bachelor Bluff, sharply, yet with a strenuous effort to be polite and deferential toward the charming young lady who had uttered this bit of philosophy—"admit it! No, madam, I deny it emphatically; in fact, I affirm there never was a more unfounded, brazen, and audacious piece of humbug."

"Really, Mr. Bluff, you are too eccentric. Does not every one say that, while man is forced to reach his conclusions by laborious processes of reasoning,

woman leaps to hers by swift and unerring intuition?"

"Yes, madam, we have been told so ceaselessly
by novelists, social essayists, and would-be philosophers of the drawing-room; in fact, the thing has
been asserted so often, that many people accept it
as a matter of course. I do not remember, indeed,
of ever hearing the assertion disputed, or of meeting in any writings of an attempt to examine its
foundations. Nevertheless, the theory is entirely
without support. There is not only not the slightest evidence in its favor, but all the facts distinctly
indicate that there is no such thing. Shall I expound, madam?—or perhaps you do not care to
hear a favorite theory ruthlessly trampled upon."

"Oh, go on, by all means, Mr. Bluff. We all
know your reputation for original notions. We must
call you the drawing-room iconoclast, for you attack all our favorite ideas."

"Let me, madam, rehearse the evidence, and then
say whether I attack favorite ideas wantonly or ignorantly. In the first place, you must see that, if
women have the power of perceiving facts or acquiring true knowledge by intuition, they are endowed with a *sixth sense*, equipped in a way that
must necessarily give them an advantage over men
in all the affairs of life. In such a case women

would be safer guides than men in almost everything, and especially in those things unsusceptible of
proof, in which we are necessarily governed by our
impressions.   Women ought to be, admitting the
theory to be true, very much better judges of character than men.   They would be furnished with
means for more prompt decision in many emergen-
cies.   They would make fewer mistakes in social
questions.   They would be better protected against
the designs of scoundrels.   They would be less susceptible to delusions of the senses, and less easily
led away by false logic.   Intuitional perceptions being the operation of a natural force, women who
possess them would not only be able to reach results sooner than men, but their conclusions would
be more sound and trustworthy—for to reason rightly requires training and experience, and consequently, while men with little experience and no training
would stumble greatly in their efforts to sift evidence and arrive at the truth, women would commonly be right off-hand.   Do you follow me, madam ? "

"Oh, yes.   So far you have shown that if women
have intuitions they are more richly endowed than
men.   Well, Mr. Bluff, that is exactly what some of
us think."

"Then, madam, if your sex is more richly endowed in this way, your intuitions ought to serve you in affairs generally. Do they? That is the test. Now, I have never been able to detect in women a special fitness for dealing with the problems of life, big or little. If women have intuitional perceptions, they ought to be very successful speculators, and, though they can not well go into Wall Street themselves, Wall Street men would be sure in such case to act solely by the advice and direction of their wives; and, if married brokers availed themselves of this power at their hand, they would soon drive bachelor brokers out of the field—or, at least, into matrimony. Every speculator with a wife would be sure, you see, of a fortune. Then, if the theory is true, no politician would ever make a move without first having consulted the intuitions of some accomplished woman. Women have sometimes acted wise parts in politics."

"And have not successful men," interrupted Miranda, "often acknowledged the great aid rendered by their wives? Recollect Lord Beaconsfield, and what he says about the service woman was to him."

"I do, madam; and I greatly honor the woman who thus upholds the ambition and great purposes of her husband. But in these occasional instances the women have possessed superior intellect and good reasoning powers; they have, you may be

sure, aided the men along the lines the men have
worked; they have helped them to their ends by
the highway of reason and judgment, and not seduced them into morasses by promises of mysterious
short cuts.   In ordinary business, just as in more
important matters, there is no evidence that intuition is worth anything, much less equal in value to
experience, or that it in any way can be substituted
for it. The trader, man or woman, who, instead of
studying the market, bought and sold by intuition,
would soon go to wreck."

"But how about domestic life?"

"In domestic life, madam, you will find that
women do not secure more trusty friends than men
do; nor are they more successful than men in selecting servants. They do not adjust themselves
more happily to the tempers and failings of com-
panions; nor more quickly perceive the consequences
of a misspoken word; nor read character more accurately; nor exhibit more insight into the future—than
the masculine sex does. In all these things there
are great differences in individuals, but there is no
evidence on record or attainable to show that the
difference separates along the line of sex; or, if the
separation is ever along the line of sex, it is against
yours, madam—simply, however, because it has less
knowledge of the world and is more impressible

than ours. It is notoriously the woman and not the man who is deceived by the soft manners and oily pretensions of the quack; it is the woman always who is overcome by the hypocritical unction of the Rev. Honeymans."

" This is a formidable array of arguments against me. I must take time to consider them."

" And yet, madam, I have not stated the most decided test of all. The most important event in the life of a woman, you will acknowledge, is the selection of a husband. In nothing else would a power of intuitional perception have a better oppor-tunity to evince itself, or be of greater service to the possessor. This may be fairly called a crucial test; and the moment it is applied the theory falls to the ground utterly. That men, who confessedly are without intuitions, often make sad mistakes in selecting their life-companions, we all know; but do they err, madam, as frequently as women do? Men are often fascinated by bad women, deluded by selfish, wrong-hearted women; but of all hope-lessly blind creatures there is none to equal a young woman enamored of an unworthy man. Sometimes it is a smooth and plausible rake; sometimes a showy, innately vulgar fellow with bad habits and atrocious tastes; sometimes a man whose fiber is coarse, and who is sure to develop into a brutal

4

and tyrannical master; sometimes it is a man whose
cold and selfish heart is for the moment concealed
under an affectation of sympathy and affection. In
whatever guise the deceiver comes, the woman, in a
majority of instances, is utterly deluded. She fails
to see the mask, or to detect the real character that
it hides. She refuses to listen to reason; she will
not believe the wise cautions of her friends; she
rejects evidence; she will not listen to admonitions
or warnings; she insists upon trusting to her intuitions, so called, and as a consequence her happiness is wrecked for life. How many woful, pitiful
tragedies have occurred in this way!"

"I declare, Mr. Bluff, you can be quite pathetic;
and you are right too, I do believe."

"Indisputably right, madam," said Mr. Bluff, rising, and walking about excitedly; "and it is monstrous for people who ought to know better to talk
of womanly intuitions in face of facts like these.
They do, I tell you, incalculable injury. Instead of
showing that reason is the only safe dependence,
that all persons must be wary of hasty impressions,
that we can not trust any guide but sound judgment, young women are brought up with the notion
that they are endowed with a special talisman, that
they possess an occult, mysterious, short-hand method of getting at facts; that they are not obliged to

sift evidence and weigh circumstances, but have only to trust implicitly to certain implanted impulses or instincts—and as a result they too frequently make appalling and irretrievable mistakes. There never was, I repeat, madam, a more unblushing and monstrous humbug than this theory of womanly intuitions, and, as it is infinitely mischievous, those who affirm it ought to be brought sharply to the bar of a revised public opinion. Do you not agree with me ? "

"I am afraid," said the lady, "that we *have* deluded ourselves in this way. Women are susceptible, quick to take impressions, very ignorant of the world, and in their ignorance supremely confident in the truth of spontaneous impressions."

" Many years ago, madam, a phrenologist assured me that I should always trust my first impressions, specially of men and women. 'You will,' he said, 'often reason yourself into another belief, and thereby be deceived; for always the idea that you instantaneously form of a person is intuitively the right one.' Well, madam, I have never forgotten the advice, and I have tested it many times; and invariably the phrenologist's theory has been wrong. I have not been and am not able to form correct judgments of men and women off-hand. First impressions have been commonly very misleading. I have found it necessary to study a man well before fully measuring and comprehending his character, and I don't believe that other people are better off in this particular than I am. I do not mean that some faces are not obviously honest and open in their character, and others dark and suspicious. Very marked tendencies are probably never concealed; but much the larger number of men and women have not distinctly marked tendencies, and these people can only be understood by some measure of familiar acquaintance."

"If you will not grant intuition to women," said the lady, "you will at least acknowledge their superiority in all matters of tact and delicate management."

" I absolutely have the temerity," replied the Bachelor, "to dispute even this theory."

"Good gracious! Mr. Bluff, will you not leave us anything?"

" A thousand admirable virtues, madam ; but as to tact you possess it equally with men in all those things in which your experiences are equal to them, and your tact is superior in all things in which your experiences are greater. Tact, I suppose, may be defined as a quick and nice discernment, a prompt perception of circumstances and facts, a ready appreciation of other people's feelings or tastes, a happy faculty in turning the corners and meeting the exigencies of social intercourse."

"In all the many minor things of the drawing-room," said Miranda, "women are invariably more ready than men. Women acquire the manners, the ease, the air of the *salon* sooner than men do; they are commonly more at home there; they are more vivacious, more sympathetic, quicker to see and act."

"This difference," replied Mr. Bluff, "is, however, more noticeable between young than between elderly people. The girl learns the art of society with ease, while the boy commonly undergoes a long and painful novitiate; but the man of maturity, when also a gentleman, has acquired social deftness in all its phases, and is master of the art usually defined as tact. While we are often called upon to admire the skill and deftness of an accomplished hostess, we shall find that an accomplished host receives his guests or presides at table with an art that is in no wise inferior. I will, however, concede that in the drawing-room women, as a rule, have more tact than men. But, when we extend our observation over a larger area, what do we discover? If we take up either domestic life, or business life, or the various organizations in which men and women gather, it is not apparent that women

are more adroit or more skillful, or that they have
nicer discernment or better perceptions than men.
I am afraid, indeed, madam, that an impartial ex-
amination of the evidence will show that, instead of
men being more insensible and less adroit than
women, they distinctly exhibit in important things
a superior skill."

"Humph! this is rather a bold defiance of accepted notions."

"Let us scan the evidence, madam, and see.
Is it not notorious that much the greater number
of domestic quarrels originate among the women of
the family? The altercations and differences that
so frequently exist between families united by marriage are almost always on the side of the women.
Men are dragged in and become partisans in the
warfare; but gauntlets are commonly first exchanged
between the ladies. Assuredly, if tact is a quality
desirable in the drawing-room as a sort of social
buffer, smoothing sharp angles and softening collisions, the very field for it is the domestic hearth,
where the unapt word, the ill-considered retort, or
the loss of self-command, is so productive of mischief. Can it be asserted that in this domain wom-
en, as a class, have more tact than men? Is peace
between husband and wife more often maintained
by the wise repression, the soft answer, the skillful

word, the adroit evasion of an issue, on the part of wives than of husbands? If we, madam, Asmodeus-like, could peep beneath the roofs of houses, which sex would we find most freely occupied in nagging? Which would we discover most commonly taking offense at the casual word? Which would be showing a superior skill in meeting and turning the dangerous little things that arise hourly in every circle? In that tact which teaches us when to hold our tongues and when to speak, what to see and what not to see, I suspect that the masculine part of the community may claim some little preëminence. Of course, I am generalizing here. We have all met with sweet-tempered wives and brutal husbands; but among the average right-intentioned people it is a deficiency of tact that so often causes collisions, and this deficiency is at least common with both sexes. Young women, my dear lady, are very skillful in managing their lovers, but many of them too frequently lose their skill when they come to manage their husbands."

"How dreadfully tiresome it must be, Mr. Bluff, to be always so exceedingly judicial!—and yet you are judicial without being just. Men are stolid and stupid; they don't quarrel because they are so intensely selfish and indifferent. Women are quicker, and more susceptible; they have warmer feelings;

they are more impulsive; they are moved sooner to righteous indignation; they are—"

"All that you say; no doubt it is more difficult for a woman to suppress her indignation, to conceal irritation, to ignore unpleasantness, to feel or affect indifference; but you see, madam, we are not inquiring into causes, but as to the fact. Women are declared to have more tact than men; so they have in some social things; but in important things I think not. It is, for instance, the lack of tact on the part of women that sets clique against clique in congregations, and in church societies of all kinds; that causes almost all associations organized by women to break up in differences; that keeps so many people in hot water in family hotels and boarding-houses, or wherever lovely woman predominates. It is to a lack of tact that we owe the traditional mother-in-law. Fathers-in-law have no bad reputations anywhere. May I not say this is because they have too much tact to interfere, too much tact to take notice of trifles, too much tact to be fussy and irritating in matters that should be wisely left alone?

"Does any woman realize how much tact men are found to exhibit in order to successfully keep their place in life? It has been shrewdly doubted, you know, whether clubs would be possible with ladies — not merely because they have not the club disposition, but because they can not abide together without getting into hostile divisions. It takes a good deal of tact to meet daily on familiar and equal terms with numerous persons, and keep all irritating things out of sight. The club is possible in the highest civilization only because nothing but the self-repression that comes of the highest social training permits men of diverse interests and tastes to come together harmoniously. The club affords an excellent test of tact; and if men are better adapted than women for club-life, if they can live together in this way without collisions, they have established the possession of tact more effectually than even the requirements of the drawing-room establish it for women.

"Then, it is impossible for one to succeed in any of the professions without the exercise of a great deal of tact. A lawyer must possess it supremely, not only in dealing with obstinate and passionate clients, but in the court-room, with judges, juries, and witnesses. A physician must possess it to a degree that only comes from a fortunate temperament and long practice. He must evade, humor, cajole, please, keep his temper, repress his impatience, hold himself well in hand, and know always how to answer questions by saying something that

means nothing. A clergyman must be endowed with
tact, or he will soon be on the rocks. He must
keep in good-humor opposing cliques, bear patiently
with ignorance and self-assertion, deal with caprice
as if it were wisdom, and know how to harmonize
the ever-ruffling matrons of his flock. The tact
that men exhibit in these ways certainly excels that
which a woman displays in managing the wholly
willing material of a dancing party or a pleasure
expedition."

"I declare, Mr. Bluff, one should never open a
subject with you until she has studied it for weeks."

"One more illustration, madam, and I have
done. The supremest exhibition of tact is to be
found in the Congressional or political leader. A
statesman representing a party or a faction is pressed
on all sides with conflicting interests, obliged to harmonize discordant materials, to be patient with impatience, to cover up the mistakes of indiscreet zeal,
to utter the timely word that heals accidental wounds,
and the appreciative word that rewards the voluntary
service; he must know when to advance upon opponents and when to withdraw; how to regulate and
adjust endless diversities of passion, ambition, selfishness, and intrigue. In men placed in these supreme
and trying situations, we often find a tact that
amounts almost to inspiration. And while it can

not be safely said that women similarly trained and similarly placed would be unequal to men, it is at least idle to talk of the superior tact of women in face of the fact that all great opportunities for the display of this talent, and all great manifestations of it, are confined exclusively to men—to the sex which it is fashionable to characterize as clumsy and blundering."

"Do you think, Mr. Bluff," said the lady, looking up into the Bachelor's face archly, "that you have shown much tact in saying all these unhandsome things about my sex to me, a woman?"

"Yes, madam, the very best tact in the world. For I counted on your good sense, and believed that with you, as with any superior woman, I could venture to speak with entire frankness and confidence."

VI

MR. BLUFF ON REALISM IN ART.

(On the Lawn, on a Summer Afternoon.)

BACHELOR BLUFF,
AN ARTIST.

Bachelor Bluff (throwing down a magazine). Really, Macbeth's " nothing is but what is not " applies to critical canons more than to anything else. Everything escapes, eludes, vanishes, is transformed under the Protean changes of critical dogmas. Do any class agree, for instance, as to what art is or what it should be? It is spiritual insight, says one; it is pure sensuousness, utters another; it is a story told to the eye, affirms a third; it is not a story at all, but a scheme of color, declares a fourth; it is a dream on canvas or in marble, says a fifth; it is the simple truth of nature, asserts some one else; it is creation; it is selecting and combining; it is technical skill plus imagination; it is joining or putting together with or without imagination;

it is — well, it seems to be whatever anybody may ingeniously suppose it to be.

Artist. Art, of course, is scientifically undefinable, just as wit and humor and other abstract qualities are. It is conceded now, however, that true art is not imitation, but creation; that it begins where imagination begins; that it is evinced by something which the artist puts into his picture from the depths of his own soul, by the beauty evolved from himself and infused into his work.

Bluff. Yes, I know. Art is not art unless it gets its head in the clouds, until it ceases to be something measurable and comprehensible, and loses itself in a mist. This is the dogma of the new æsthetic and ecstatic school. Giving the school all the respect that by the utmost stretch is its due, all that can be said is that this is the definition of sensuous imaginative art. I say sensuous imaginative, for all this transcendental art is, at bottom, of the earth, earthy—it is ultra-sensuous, an intoxication of color and form. A definition of art that embraces only a part of the facts, that excludes nineteen twentieths of the things that are commonly included in art, is certainly as arbitrary as it is inadequate. There are imaginative art, graphic art, picturesque art, decorative art, and the average man has no difficulty whatever in determining what things belong

to art and what do not. It is only when a mind
of unscientific training feels called upon to define,
that confusion ensues. And this confusion arises
mainly from confounding *degree* with *kind*, as there
are people who insist that poetry means something
exalted, whereas it only means a definite form of
literary expression. It is not imagination, nor imagery, nor beauty, that distinguishes poetry from
prose, but simply metrical arrangement. In the
same way it is not imagination, nor mystery, nor
spirituality, nor exaltation of any kind, that makes
art, for these things relate only to degree and
quality, to certain phases of art. Art begins at the
beginning; it is in the rude sculpture of the Egyp-
tian or the Aztec, in the tentative and often grotesque efforts of the earliest painters, in the crude
sketch of the novice.   •

Artist. But art assuredly must mean performance,
and not mere attempt at performance. It must have
some significance, some thought, some appeal to the
higher feelings. It must reveal to us forms of
beauty, and awaken in us spiritual pleasure. If
your idea is pushed to the extreme, then art must
include every form of mere mechanical execution,
every piece of unimaginative literalism, every form
of feeble manipulation. No one will assent to your
judgment. Art begins this side of mechanism, and

this side of every form of literalism; its essential quality is—

Bluff. What? That is the whole question. If we can find the essential quality of art, the indisputable something the presence of which can be detected, we shall have a definition of art.

Artist. Is it not beauty?

Bluff. Beauty covers a vast field in art, and we often hear it declared to be its real purpose. The real purpose of art is not so easily ascertained. That beauty is not the essential quality of art is evident from the fact that very ugly scenes in nature have been painted with such vigor and skill as to fairly captivate the beholder. Some of the French landscapists will fascinate you with a marsh, a few stunted, deformed trees, and a sky. A symmetrical tree gives us the lines of beauty, but there isn't an artist anywhere that doesn't prefer twisted, misshapen trees to symmetrical ones. There is more character in them, he will say. But yet character does not make art. Some artists with us seem fairly to detest beauty. They wish to be bold, strong, virile; and they appear to delight in ugliness. The impressionists think themselves preëminently artists, yet their claims to art lie in the exclusion of form, of color, of meaning, and of every suggestion of beauty—as beauty is commonly understood. No;

beauty is only one factor in art. Art may awaken sensations of awe or of sympathy; it may be weird, gaunt, grotesque, and melancholy; it may deal with storm, turbulence, anger, passion, death. It has, in fact, the whole field of expression, and is as catholic as life and the world.

Artist. I do not dispute its range of expression, although art continually makes excursions into fields where it does not legitimately belong. But, while the range of expression may be wide, the range of performance has its limits. Not every one who says " I am an artist " really reaches to art.

Bluff. To worthy art, I grant. But I wish to scrutinize this notion that art begins somewhere with the beginning of the ideal. When I turn over an artist's portfolios I find scores of sketches—now the trunk of a tree, now a head or figure, now a mass of rocks, now a study of a ruin, now a bit of coast. Are these things not art? Meissonier once, when dining, caught up a burned match and, half forgetfully, began drawing a figure on the tablecloth. The host quietly thrust other burned matches in his way; and so spirited was the figure drawn in this spontaneous way that the delighted host afterward had the cloth framed. Was not this sketch art? Are not Détaille's single military figures art? Are not Tenniel's cartoons and Du Maurier's capital social sketches in "Punch" to be considered as art? Is not an etching by Haden or Unger art? Is not an Etruscan vase, a piece of majolica ware, an old bit of *repoussé* silver-work, a piece of carving by Gibbons, art? Come, where will you draw the line?

Artist. By a cheap license of speech, art covers almost everything that people desire to make it cover. There are art tailors and art boot-makers, you know. A term that is made to mean everything soon ceases to mean anything. I must insist upon it that art, in its fullness and completeness, means imaginative and creative putting together. I have no inclination to consider the innumerable idle things that borrow its name.

Bluff. In one sense you are right. There is imaginative work in all genuine art, but it is that power of imagination which enables one to see things as they are, and grasp all the facts. Realism is absolutely a very high order of imagination. Look, now, at yonder group of trees, with tints just glinting their upper branches as presage of the coming sunset. You will say, perhaps, that copying those trees would be mechanical and not art work. And yet, to copy them as they are, to catch their grace, their form, their lines, their tints, their play of light and shade, their hundred vivid characteristics, could never be done by a cold, mechanical mind. To

paint those trees the artist must penetrate them, appropriate them, master them. The forces within him
must stir, his mind must awaken, his eye be full of
alertness, his soul open itself to their unspeakable
fascinations, his whole being glow with a sense of
their wonders. And I tell you there is not a rock,
a tree, a branch, a flower, a hillside, a sweep of
wave, a play of light, a touch of color, that, if reproduced with all its expression in form and tint,
would not delight you. The painter need not draw
upon his imagination by an atom. The thing itself,
if it is the whole, true, full thing, is enough. And
observe, all cold or mechanical copying never gets
within a hundred degrees of the real facts. Do you
think that it would be mere mechanism, mere deftness of hand, to draw the horse in the meadow beyond us? Mere deftness would give you nothing
more than a wooden horse. It takes the very highest skill to give the lines, the sense of power, the
truth of motion, the real life of the animal—and it
has never yet been done by any one whose pencil
was not guided by imaginative force. "The perception of beauty and power in whatever objects or
in whatever degree they subsist," says Hazlitt, "is
the test of real genius." So you see there *is* imagination in art; not the imagination that certain writers mean, not the dreaming that strives for the light

that never was on sea or land, but the immense force and susceptibility that master and possess the light that *is* on sea and land.

Artist. This is making realism a branch of imagination, facts as potent as poetry, things that are as exalted as things that we dream.

Bluff. For my part, I haven't the slightest objection to people seeing visions, but prefer that they should begin by seeing facts. The sculptor who translates all the thousand expressions that exist in the human figure will rival the Greek Phidias; the landscapist who possesses himself with all the facts of nature will outdo all his competitors. I point again to my group of trees; who will come and paint them?—not feebly and vaguely, but reproduce them in all their splendor. Who will do it? You would find a hundred idealists to one with perceptions and hand vigorous enough for the task. Idealism is in fact the cheapest thing in the world; so far from its being that which cultivated people only can comprehend, as the critics are constantly assuming, it is distinctly the thing that the crude, untrained public admire. See the wide fame of Doré. Here is an artist that, in black-and-white at least, meets all the theoretical requirements of your school. He has immense fecundity, boundless resources, and affluent imagination; he is utterly regardless of nature or

truth, securing his effects by the most audacious exaggeration—and yet, while the public delight in his
work, it is quite the fashion among artists and critics to sneer at it. His exuberant imagination leads
him to extravagance, to theatrical sensation, to
strained and untruthful delineations, to endless violence to the simplicity and truth of nature. And
these things, which, if your set is right, ought to be
virtues, are things which the better informed sum
up against him as sins. They are of a character,
let me say, which in the constitution of the human
mind are sure to mark all affluent and over-teeming
minds. The susceptible and uncritical public find
pleasure in these manifestations of power, but acute
and cultured people prefer the modest beauty of
nature. Then there is Bouguereau. It has become
quite the fashion recently to sneer at this painter
because his flesh-tints are so smooth, so merely
pretty and refined, so devoid of robust vigor and
vivid truth. Obviously these fault-finders are all
wrong. It is not truth that is wanted. Bouguereau's
imagination is on the side of sweet tints, of ideal
grace and delicacy; he paints nude figures through
a haze of tender beauty. What right have any of
us to complain, however lacking in virile force his
work may be? Great artists are not realists, say
the critics—they do not paint, says Hamerton, what

is but what is *not.* Hence, in Bouguereau's paintings, we must accept the artist's conception of flesh,
not flesh as we know it and see it.

Artist. Every truly great painter paints nature
not as it is, but as it enters his imagination. Art
ceases to be art by becoming imitation.

Bluff. This word *imitation* is very confusing and
misleading. If by imitation is meant *deceptive* imitation—the painting of objects with such servile fidelity as to deceive one into the belief that he is looking
upon real things—the thing is paltry enough. But
I do not use the word imitation. Drawing the outlines of a tree, according to Ruskin, is not imitating a
tree, but giving the *form* of a tree. The question is
between nature sweetened and idealized, as a man
may sleepily dream it, or nature seized upon with all
the force and spring of the mind, so as to make it
captivatingly faithful. Now, one who paints nature
as he sees it paints it as it is so far as he can realize it; if he does not see it as it is, his vision is
abnormal, and assuredly this unfits him for the vocation. If he consciously paints it as it is not, painting it neither as it is nor as he sees it, what have
we, then, but an artist substituting a fancy, a notion, a perverse and intentional fallacy, for the veri-
ties of creation? Such notions might in some instances be good, but have they any just reason for

their being, and could they be more glorious than great Nature? And then, just as sure as we admit the principle that an artist may paint his own conceptions as nature, we shall open the door for every conceivable outcome of vanity, foolishness, and grotesque fancy—such as would soon cast art into a pit of darkness and delirium.

Artist. A majority of painters see only the surface of things; they depict the beauty of the external world exclusively, being wholly insensible to the soul of nature, which it is the true province of genius to depict and express.

Bluff. Yes; of course if there are painters who are spokesmen of the external aspects of nature only, and others who are prophets of its internal spirit, then the latter must obviously be much greater artists. But what is this internal spirit? How is it separated from outside phenomena? What are the special qualities not revealed in surfaces that certain gifted men discover and express? Let us see if we can penetrate beneath the surface of this theory. When any one is contemplating a scene in nature, he is impressed by the variety and beauty of *form*, by the infinite gradations and felicitous contrasts of *color*, by the vivid effects of *light* and *shadow*, by the rich differences of *texture*, by the mellowing influences of the *atmosphere*, by a sense of expansion that comes from *space.* These are the things that every artist studies and endeavors to reproduce; and the success of the painter in each case will depend upon his skill in mastering relatively all the different conditions presented to him. If he enters too minutely into every detail, his picture, by the multiplication of particulars, will, as a whole, lose all resemblance; if he omits those particulars that are necessary to make up the sense of the whole, his picture will lack truth and virility. The artist must have a strong capacity for seeing all that is before him, and an artistic perception that enables him to decide rightly the separate circumstances that he must either reject or subordinate. If he is of a cold, dull mind, he works patiently on, photographically copying what he sees; if he is of an imaginative, susceptible nature, he seizes salient beauties, he gives full value to an effect here, he suppresses one there, he throws into the composition ideas drawn from former experiences. But what possible thing can he put on his canvas that is not a "report of surfaces"? He begins with form; no man can invent lines or combinations of lines that are not in nature, and they have no possible characteristics that are not external. He proceeds to color, and is here so bewildered and embarrassed by the richness of nature, the exquisite gradations that no skill can

master, the overwhelming loveliness of tints that his
pigments can only hint at, that he is in despair—
but color, nevertheless, is a thing of surfaces. He
next struggles with texture. How can he suggest
the tooth of the rock, the edge of the bark, the
porcelain of the rose, is his problem—and texture is
the very crust of things, beyond which it is not his
mission to penetrate. Light and shade, and atmosphere, are simply external things that modify other
external things, that either soften or make contrasts, define or blend lines, articulate foregrounds
or mellow distances. If after form, color, texture,
light and shade, atmosphere, and space—all being
external aspects — there are other conditions, what
are they? How is the " soul of things " expressed
otherwise than by obvious phenomena? If a thing
is not obvious, how is it detected? Are there spiritual landscapes similar to the alleged spiritual pho-
tographs? Is the soul of things a ghost that prophets or seers only can behold? In the group of trees
we have been studying there is marvelous beauty:
remove light and shade, and the picture becomes
dull; extinguish color, and its charm has almost
gone; obliterate interlacing lines, and it is charac-
terless; but it seems there is a soul left. Well, this
soul must be the sort of divinity that we see in a
telegraph-pole or a wood-pile! No; it is certain

that there is no internal soul of things separable from the aspects of things; the difference we find in the works of painters is not an imaginary line of this character—it is the difference of power, the difference between one who sees and comprehends vigorously and one who feebly or only half sees, the difference between susceptibility and unsusceptibility. Instead of a painter inventing a nature of his own, trying to see things in lights and under aspects different from the way other people see them, his real mission is to passionately study nature, to penetrate it, to take possession of it, to enter into its subtilties, to master its mysteries, to see it with the heart and soul as well as with the eye, in order that he may reproduce it intense, powerful, virile, glorious!

Artist. The conflict between imaginative art and realistic art is not likely to be soon settled, and each man judges, doubtless, as he feels. But we started with the purpose of defining art, and have drifted greatly. Can we find a definition that is likely to be generally acceptable?

Bluff. The definition should be broad enough to cover the whole, or nearly the whole field, and that includes indispensable elements. How would it do to say that art *is form, or form and color so combined or expressed as to awaken sensations of pleasure?*

Artist. I do not think this will do. Vulgar form

5

or color may, for instance, awaken sensations of pleasure in vulgar minds, and very good form or color fails to impress stupid and insensible minds.

Bluff. I am well aware that it is not a perfect or complete definition, such a definition as would enable one always, by applying it, to determine whether any given performance is art or not. It would be impossible, moreover, to define art so as to enlighten vulgar or stupid minds. But it is a definition that covers a tolerably wide range of conditions, and it is one which, if accepted, would stop a good deal of current nonsense—the nonsense that sets up a set of narrow dogmas and aims to turn out of the pale everybody's ideas and performances that do not coincide with them. It permits the ideal and includes the graphic; it recognizes pretty nearly the whole range of work usually characterized as art.

Artist. Have you not said that art deals with awe, sympathy, turbulence, passion, and death?

Bluff. These may be its themes; but form and color are the media through which these things are expressed, and determine the art-character of the work—sometimes too much so, for the conception of an event is often overlooked by artists in considering exclusively the technical treatment. However, if you do not like my definition, frame a better one.

VII

MR. BLUFF DISCOURSES OF THE COUN- TRY AND KINDRED THEMES.

(In a Country Lane.)

BACHELOR BLUFF.
A LISTENER.

—— "THE country," exclaimed Mr. Bluff, with an air of candor and impartiality, "is, I admit, a very necessary and sometimes a very charming place. I thank Heaven for the country when I eat my first green peas, when the lettuce is crisp, when the potatoes are delicate and mealy, when the well-fed poultry comes to town, when the ruddy peach and the purple grape salute me at the fruit-stands. I love the country when I think of a mountain ramble; when I am disposed to wander with rod and reel along the forest-shadowed brook; when the apple-orchards are in blossom; when the hills blaze with autumn foliage. But I protest against the dogmatism of rural people, who claim all the cardinal and all the remaining virtues for their rose-beds and cabbage-patches. The town, sir, bestows felicities higher in character than the country does; for men and women, and the works of men and women, are always worthier our love and concern than the rocks and the hills. Contact with mind, with imagination, with fancy, with ideas and aspirations and discussions, with men of wit and purpose and intellectual life, is worth to the mind and to character more than dumb Nature at her best can bestow. That is the best-fortified soul which has experienced the fullness of town and the sweetness of country life; but nothing can be more absurd than the airs of superior moral and mental status which suburban folk so often assume. Life must be largely enriched with those experiences that pertain to a metropolis before one can be fully capable of enjoying the charms of rural retirement. Men must have the ceaseless friction of mankind in order to live ripely and develop fully. There have been great men and lovable men who have proclaimed their preference for these paved concourses of men. No man can justly accuse me of trivial tastes with the example of old Dr. Johnson before him; and who would not have rather walked down Fleet Street with the honest old Ursa Major than sit droning and dozing for a decade under a vine and fig-tree? And heroic Charles Lamb! Who may not love the shop-windows, the chop-houses, the theatres, the book-stalls, the town-sights of all sorts, when the noble Elia has wandered through and among them, drawing the happiest images, the most playful humor; the rarest fancy, the sweetest sentiments from them? After Charles Lamb all men may rise up and bless the streets! And then have we not also delightful Leigh Hunt and witty Douglas Jerrold in the ranks of the town's defenders? And then there are Dickens and Thackeray. If ever spirits haunted the places they loved, these devoted chroniclers of town-life hover above and mingle amid the crowds it was once their delight to study and depict. You may be sure, sir, that insensibility to the active and stirring aspects of the town arises from dullness of imagination. All the brighter and more impressible spirits have almost invariably preferred the contact of men to the solitude of Nature; and this preference will continue, you may be certain, so long as people delight in the refinements of society and the fruits of civilization.

—— " Oh, yes! I have heard before of the pleasures of the garden. Poets have sung, enthusiasts have written, and old men have dreamed of them since History began her chronicles. But have

the *pains* of the garden ever been dwelt upon ?
Have people, now, been entirely honest in what
they have said and written on this theme? When
enthusiasts have told us of their prize pears, their
early peas of supernatural tenderness, their aspara-
gus, and their roses, and their strawberries, have
they not hidden a good deal about their worm-
eaten plums—about their cherries that were carried
off by armies of burglarious birds; about their potatoes that proved watery and unpalatable; about
their melons that fell victims to their neighbors'
fowls; about their peaches that succumbed to the
unexpected raid of Jack Frost; about their grapes
that fell under the blight of mildew; about their
green corn that withered in the hill; about the
mighty host of failures that, if all were told, would
tower in high proportion above the few much-
blazoned successes ?

"Who is it that says a garden is a standing
source of pleasure? Amend this, I say, by asserting that a garden is a standing source of discomfort and vexation. There is always something in
the garden to be done or planned, always something to be reconstructed or readjusted. The car-
penter is in perpetual demand with the man who
has a garden. So is the mason. So is the florist.
So is the laborer. So is the machinist. A man

with a garden is always trying to accomplish the impracticable. He is always planning how he can unite a maximum of sunshine with a maximum of shade; how he can keep his trees, and yet open distant prospects; how he can enlarge his stables without abridging his grounds ; how he can shut out an ugly view in one direction and reveal a pretty one in another; how he can expand his vegetable-beds, and yet keep them hidden behind his flower-parterres; how he can curve and lengthen a path in order to make his estate appear larger, or straighten it, so as to add to his convenience; how he can best keep his paths in order; what should be done to improve the appearance of his lawn; how he can save his shrubs that are threatened with decay; how he can rescue his fruit-trees from the insects; how he can keep off the mosquitoes and prevent the ague! His devices, and his designs, and his experiments, are legion. A hopeless restlessness, according to my observation, takes possession of every amateur gardener. Discontent abides in his soul. There is, indeed, so much to be done, changed, rearranged, watched, nursed, that the amateur gardener is really entitled to praise and generous congratulations when one of his thousand schemes comes to fruition. We ought in pity to rejoice with him over his big Lawton blackberries, and say nothing of the cherries, and the pears, and the peaches, that once were budding hopes, but have gone the way of Moore's 'dear gazelle.' Then the large expenditures which were needed to bring about his triumph of the Lawtons. 'Those potatoes,' said an enthusiastic amateur gardener to me once, 'cost twenty-five cents apiece!' And they were very good potatoes, too—almost equal to those that could be bought in market at a dollar a bushel.

"And then, amateur gardeners are feverishly addicted to early rising. Men with gardens are like those hard drinkers whose susceptibilities are hopelessly blunted. Who but a man diverted from the paths of honest feeling and natural enjoyment, possessed of a demoniac mania, lost to the peace and serenity of the virtuous and the blessed, could find pleasure amid the damps, and dews, and chills, and raw-edgedness of a garden in the early morning, absolutely find pleasure in saturated trousers, in shoes swathed in moisture, in skies that are gray and gloomy, in flowers that are, as Mantalini would put it, 'demnition moist'? The thing is incredible! Now, a garden, after the sun has dried the paths, warmed the air, absorbed the dew, is admissible. But a possession that compels an early turning out into fogs and discomforts deserves for this fact alone the anathema of all rational beings.

"I really believe, sir, that the literature of the garden, so abundant everywhere, is written in the interest of suburban land-owners. The inviting one-sided picture so persistently held up is only a covert bit of advertising, intended to seduce away happy cockneys of the town — men supremely contented with their attics, their promenades in Fifth Avenue, their visits to Central Park, where all is arranged for them without their labor or concern, their evenings at the music gardens, their soft morning slumbers which know no dreadful chills and dews! How could a back-ache over the pea-bed compensate for these felicities? How could sour cherries, or half-ripe strawberries, or wet rose-buds, even if they do come from one's own garden, reward him for the loss of the ease and the serene conscience of one who sings merrily in the streets, and cares not whether worms burrow, whether suns burn, whether birds steal, whether winds overturn, whether droughts destroy, whether floods drown, whether gardens flourish, or not?

——— "Yesterday I read an article in 'Blackwood' on 'Weather,' in which the writer, who seems to admire almost everything in Nature, makes an assault on fog. Yes, sir, fog. He denounces it as stagnant, sulky, and silent; as hopelessly objectionable, ugly, useless, stupid, and dirty. Now, sir, it is simply amazing how a writer, who delights ' in richly-endowed but widely wayward Nature,' should utter this wholly wrongful judgment upon one of 'the family of weather' that to the observant eye has, not less than its kindred, its strange surprises, its picturesque aspects, its manifold beauties. Fog may be dirty in the cities when mixed with and stained by smoke, and at times it is undoubtedly stagnant, if not stupid; but one who has watched the movements of fog, who has seen the endless number of dissolving views it forms, who has noted the striking and picturesque ways in which artists use it, must resent the unhandsome epithets of our 'Blackwood' writer. Have you ever passed a summer vacation on the seashore, and, stretching yourself upon a headland of the shore, watched the vagaries and fantastic sports of the soft, subtile, and undulating fog; how it now comes rolling in from the sea with swift and steady course, first obscuring the horizon, then swallowing up sail after sail; next seizing upon jutting points of land, sweeping along the sides of the cliffs, until suddenly it takes possession of and blots out the whole surface of sea and land? Then presently you see a blue space overhead; all at once a shadowy sail looms through the mist; the fog lifts and shows a stretch of calm sea; then

as suddenly again, as if some prompter regulated
the rise and fall of this strange curtain, down falls
the drapery of mist, and everything is hidden !
These shiftings and changes make striking pictures,
believe me.   At one moment a sail suddenly appears, without a hull, dark, shadowy, and mystic in
its body, but with its upper line catching the sunlight and glittering white like the wing of some
huge bird of the sea ; in an instant more the fog
has seized upon the sail, and enveloped it wholly,
but the mantle is lifted beneath so as to reveal the
dark form of the hull.   If there are points of wooded
headland jutting into the sea, you look and see
them wholly obscured, but even while you look a
long line of trees appears above a mass of drifting
mist, looking like forests hung in the heavens.   I
once watched pictures like these, forming and dissolving continually, and hence, I say, that he must
be strangely ignorant of the mystic sprite called fog
who heaps upon it such epithets as I have quoted.
There is no better scenic artist on sea or land, sir,
than the fog on a summer day when the winds un-
steadily come and go.

—— " The picturesque ! We talk a good deal
about the picturesque, but how many of us understand what it is ?   No, sir ; we like to boast of our

mountains, our cascades, our lakes, our forests, our rivers; every summer the avenues of travel are crowded with throngs of pilgrims in search of what they call the picturesque; and yet, if there were any true natural sense of the picturesque, it would be sure to be exhibited in the houses we build. Look at the villas, mansions, cottages, what-not, that ambition and wealth multiply all around us, and see how rarely we find anything picturesque, or even really pleasing to an artistic eye. The big villas and pinchbeck cottages that abound in our suburbs completely outrage every idea of the picturesque; in fact, we are never so hopelessly unpicturesque as when we are endeavoring to be picturesque. What people really like is prettiness. They want ornamented towers, Mansard-roofs, fresh paint, white walls, showy gardens, and strange novelties of all kinds—caster-boxes, pagodas, gilt cages, Swiss toys, an interminable range of fantastic devices, whose names no man knoweth. No one seems to have an idea of building a house that will look as if it grew a part of the landscape, but must set it like a glittering paste-jewel on a soiled finger, an abominable contrast with its surroundings. Then see how cold and uninhabitable most of the better kind of country places seem in their spotless lawns, their shrubbery trimmed to an extreme of cold propriety, their

dreary gravel-walks, their distant and reserved air,
their whole atmosphere of restraint and human emptiness! There is no life, no soul, no heartiness, no
hospitality, no sense of comfort or felicity in those
mausoleums, in which are buried human interests and
passions. Many a humble cottage is a thousand
times more inviting. I can not imagine myself
living in them or dreaming in them; of finding in
them life, or repose, or any form of human sweetness. When you build, sir, build with less pretension, with better sense of mellow contrasts and
quiet tones; let nature be a little free, and art a
little modest; give to your country domicile the air
of a rustic lass, coy and modest, and not the flash
and cold disdain of a town belle.

—— " I wonder many times whether Nature feels
any delight in man; whether it is insensible to the
human affections offered to it. When the sea has
all the winter months beat its dull, sad refrain
upon the beach, does it not curl its white locks
in graceful and joyous anticipation when it knows
that youth and beauty are soon again to resume
their places on the sands? Does it not feel longing in its winter loneliness for the merriment of
the summer sea-bathers? Can it not delight in
the laughing girls and handsome boys that come

down to sport in its old arms? Have the woods
no kindly sympathy with our pleasure in their silent shades? Can not the mountains feel a glowing pride in our admiration for their stately majesty? We can at least imagine the mountains
and the woods and the sea waiting with earnest
welcome for us, in the great largeness of their an-
tique soul opening wide their bosom to the pulse of
human feeling. This notion, you see, simply trans-
fers to Nature something of the old Greek personality; it makes Pan live again; it restores the Dry-
ads to the woods and the Naiads to the waters.

—— "The beauty of every scene, my good sir,
depends on the altitude of the sun and the angle
of light. What is a mountain at high noon but a
lumpish, dead, meaningless mass? But see the same
mountain later in the day, with the sun behind it,
and you have a magnificent picture. It stands in
superb purple against a sky radiant with gold and
yellow, like a crowned monarch at a pageant. But
it does not need a mountain to make a picture;
sky and sunshine and air will do it for us anywhere. There was a time, and that only recently,
when artists went forth hunting for scenes to paint
—they searched for the weird, the terrible, the grotesque, the strange, the remote, the picturesque, the

imposing, the unfamiliar, and all the while left con-
summate pictures at their very doors! Our later
painters have found this out; they take a plain, a
meadow with a stunted tree, a stretch of sand and
sea, a clump of trees, any simple scene, and paint
the light that falls upon it, the sky that overarches
it, the atmosphere that fills it, and the picture stands
a thing of beauty. Light and air, which are everywhere, are everything. I remember once standing
just at sunset on the northern shore of Long Island
Sound. The sun was behind me, with all the eastern sky glowing with the reflected light of the west-
ern pageant, which was hid from me by a stretch
of forest-trees. There was no wind, and the wide
expanse of the Sound, as smooth, polished, and placid
as a mirror, caught on its surface an exquisite pink
tint from the sky above it. On this pink sea there
were several becalmed vessels, whose sails stood
yellow against the sky, with the hulls in shadow,
like masses of dark bronze—all being perfectly reflected in the glassy surface upon which they hung
suspended. Well, sir, it was a picture that an artist
like Gifford would have delighted to paint, and yet
it was but a momentary effect of light. One need
not leave the town even to see these phantasmago-
ria of the heavens. Who has ever painted the light
of the setting sun on the house-tops, on gables, and

chimneys, and dormer-windows? I have seen it, sir, make our commonplace brick walls look like the domes and pinnacles of a celestial city. There are rare bits of scene-painting of this kind in town, if you only know how to look for them.

—— " Pleasure, you say! Pleasure-seeking, sir, commonly ends in more pain than delight. Our felicities are coy and wayward; they come we know not whence, we can never be sure how, but often, when most desired or most vigorously sought for, they fail to respond, and quite as often, when least anticipated, they fill us with their glory. Pleasure can not be successfully prearranged. Too many conditions are necessary. One may sometimes secure everything but the disposition to enjoy, or he may find that the very fact of deliberately determining to be happy is of itself sufficient to destroy all possibility of happiness. Then many forms of pleasure are a violent assault upon happiness. People seem to think that felicity is garrisoned in a citadel, and that due energy will be sure to conquer and secure the prize. Pleasure is in truth a jack-o'-lantern that we pursue only to see it escape us; or it is a frail, delicate blossom, invisible in the gay *parterre* set out ostentatiously in its name, but appearing sometimes suddenly at our very feet in the ordinary highway where we looked for weeds only; or, again, it is a little spirited cherub that avoids the glare of noisy shows, and all form of loud pretension, but in quiet hours slips into our heart and sets it beating with strange ecstasy. Premeditated pleasure, sir, is as impossible as premeditated wit. One can not sit down and say, 'I will make a jest'; he can not rise up and say, 'I will go and find pleasure.' Every summer we see all our towns, all our summer resorts, all our hotels, all our highways, full of violent seekers after pleasure. Men are hurrying for it to the seashore, pursuing it up the mountains, angling for it in the lakes, dancing for it at the watering-places, sailing for it on the rivers, rushing for it on the railways, fatiguing themselves almost to death for it everywhere—and yet rarely finding it. He is the happiest who knows how to extract pleasure from the thousand little things that lie in his daily path—from the sunshine and the rain, from the grass and the trees, from flowers and books, from old friends and new faces, from crowds and from solitude; who knows how to note the shifting panorama of life that ceaselessly offers him change and contemplation, and does not imagine that pleasure must be sought with drum and trumpet and boisterous expectation.

—— " Does any one ever sit down when the

summer is over and compare his two expeditions to
the country—yes, sir, his two expeditions—one the
trip that he expected to take, and the other the
trip that he really did take? We all of us generally
lay out in advance, on these occasions, a very hopeful and attractive programme; and we are apt to
end with a performance in which a good many
changes have to be made. For weeks beforehand
we furbish up our fishing-rods; we clean the fowl-
ing-piece ; we put ourselves in order in various
ways for the long tramp, the sail, the ride, the picnic, the angling excursion; and we say to ourselves
that our pleasure shall not be abridged by the want
of forethought or the need of preparation. And yet
how differently matters turn out ! The picnic to
the seashore would have been a great success had
not the roads been so unendurably hot and dusty;
the tide, by a miscalculation of somebody, so low;
and threatening showers made an early rush homeward so necessary. The long-planned yachting excursion, in which fine winds, careening sails, exhilarating life in the swiftly-coursing yacht, were so
eagerly prepictured, must of course fall on a day
when a dead calm rendered motion almost impossible. The sails clung to the mast, the vessel drifted
a little with the tide, and the long, dull hours were
spent wistfully hoping for a breeze. And then how

delightful the angling was going to be! One saw himself wandering along picturesque little rivers, under arching trees, and by little, charming cascades. He fancied himself casting the fly into the silent, shaded pool, and saw the splendid dash with which some veteran of the brook darted at the skillfully-dropped bait. He pictured the splendid and well-managed battle with the fish, and imagined it triumphantly landed. He saw himself, after a superb day's sport, wending homeward with his basket, bending under the weight of his day's victories. But always that tremendous difference between calculation and realization! The picturesque little stream proved to be half dried up; the cascades were only threads of water; the trees let in the hot and scorching sun; in the dark pools no trout rose to the fly; and the journey homeward was with an empty basket, a hungry stomach, jaded limbs, and muttered maledictions on fly-fishing generally. One's other attempts at pleasure-making also exhibited a difference between anticipation and performance. The mountain scenery was not so fine and exhilarating as was expected. The watering-places were either half attended and dull, or overcrowded and uncomfortable. All stay-at-homes, those who take only one trip to the country, and that the imaginary one, may console themselves that they have no

disappointments of the kind to mourn over. There
are always compensations, you see, if we have the
wisdom to discover them.

—— " How intolerably hot it is! There is need,
sir, of an entire change in our notions of summer.
This season has, in all ages, and probably among all
peoples, been the popular type of felicity. Not only
has poetry in a thousand ways dwelt upon its charms
and sung of its beauties, but proverbs have epito-
mized its delights, and it has served to symbolize
other forms of peace, happiness, and fruition. We
count youth and beauty by summers; peevish and
wrinkled old age by winters. Our discontents, our
harsher passions, our evil fortunes, are often graph-
ically paralleled by the rude aspects of December
and January, while our contents and all our felicities are continually symbolized in the soft conditions of summer. Now, sir, this exaltation of the
summer solstice has much more justification in tradition than in experience. When the world was
young, no doubt, the summer season was justly entitled to all the appreciation it enjoyed — all the
bountiful praise and admiration now bestowed upon
it by poets. Then, art did not know how to miti-
gate the severities of winter, and civilization supplied no resources for enjoyment in the long, sun-

less hours. Then, with summer came abundance, while winter was always associated with stint and deprivation. Fruits, that art could not preserve, were enjoyed only during the brief period in which they ripened. The harvest brought its plenty, but human ingenuity had not devised methods for extending it throughout the year. Consequently, in primitive conditions the summer meant fruition and beneficence far more significantly than it does now. The abundance which we enjoy could not exist, it is true, if the summer suns did not do their work; but the enjoyment of summer plenty is not now essentially identified with the season, as it was in early and rude periods of civilization. So there is implanted in our hereditary instincts, treasured up in our traditions, imbedded in our language, a vast deal of matter pertaining to summer which needs in these latter times to be revised. Civilization, which has deprived winter of all its terrors, and which has even converted some of its harshest features into means of enjoyment, has not succeeded at all with the discomforts of summer; so that, if we were governed less by tradition and more by actual experience, we would be disposed to look upon summer as a period necessary to be endured, in order that harvests may ripen, rather than as one within itself essentially felicitous. The heats of sum-

mer suns prostrate us. The dust borne upon summer airs suffocates us. The fevers bred by summer
poisons sicken us. In fact, excessive heat causes an
aggregate of suffering which cold can not parallel.
The stirring winds of winter invigorate rather than
destroy; or, if they prove too harsh and severe, our
warm houses and our abundant clothing give us
ample protection. Ordinarily the air of winter gives
us strength and spirit, and the energy that succumbs
entirely to the torrid suns of July will be aroused
to a martial glow in a manly encounter with the
December gale. I doubt even if the destitute suffer
more in winter than in summer. Nothing seems so
terrible as those streets of New York occupied by
tenement-houses on hot summer days; I have visited
them in the different seasons, and the inmates really
appear to suffer more in July from heat, want of
fresh air, insects, and sickness, than in winter from
cold and exposure. If people would be honest they
would confess that they endure the summer rather
than enjoy it. Those who remain in our cities
pant and stifle, and long for the return of winter;
those who, in the name of pleasure, go in search of
boasted summer delights, are scorched on mountain-
tops, choked in dust-filled cars and stage-coaches,
burned on exposed seacoasts, and assaulted everywhere by mosquitoes and other insects. Art has

mitigated, sir, and civilization conquered, all other seasons but summer; and it is quite time that poetry and the common sentimental utterance of the country were animated by facts as they are, and not by traditions founded on conditions of things long past.

VIII

MR. BLUFF ON THE PRIVILEGES OF WOMEN.

(On the Promenade.)

BACHELOR BLUFF,
A LADY.

—— "*The right of women to intellectual activity!*
In the name of reason, madam, who has denied the
right of women to intellectual activity? There are
no laws and no restrictions, legal, moral, or social,
that restrain women's intellectual activity. They
may, at their pleasure—limited, of course, by their
natural capacity—become philosophers, poets, novelists, historians, essayists, journalists, scientists, naturalists, inventors, painters, sculptors, musicians, singers, composers, lecturers, actors; they may become
famous as thinkers, distinguished as conversationalists,
and renowned for learning. Books are open to
them, Nature is open to them; in society they are
absolute queens. They may acquire all the wisdom

of the ancients and the moderns; they may search
out the mysteries of life and Nature; they may give
to social intercourse an intellectual elevation it has
hitherto never known.

—— "*If they had the opportunity!*   Madam, this
is the ceaseless cry, but women absolutely have more
opportunity than men.   Not so many of them have
the advantage of college education, it is true, but
the greatest achievements in philosophy, science, invention, art, and literature, have been made by men
who never saw the inside of a college.   Men of
strong purpose create opportunity for themselves—
create it while weaker minds are lamenting the obstacles that lie in their way.   As for relative opportunity between the sexes, nearly all men are condemned either to business or the professions, and
from an early age all their energies are thus bent
in one enforced direction, while many women—not
all, of course — have exceptional freedom in the
choice of their studies and pursuits.   All the preva-
lent fuss and fret pertaining to this question comes,
madam, from those women who are wholly without
intellectual activity, but who are burned up with
diseased vanity, and imagine that there are royal
roads to distinction which the men enjoy and the
other sex are debarred from.

6

—— "*Women can not be lawyers, judges, or statesmen!* No, madam, they can not yet. But no one
who comprehends the subject would dream of calling exclusions of this character a limitation of intellectual activity. Law, medicine, and politics, which
these restless women hunger for, are really the last
pursuits that one with genuine 'intellectual activity'
would think of following. The irksome and exacting duties of these professions keep the individual
on a tread-mill; they prevent study, they narrow the
line of thought,. they render almost impossible that
altitude of pure intellectuality which the suppressed
female genius of the land thirsts for. Business, as I
have said, so generally imposed upon men in America, to the great injury of their higher faculties,
is not imposed upon women, and hence many of
the 'subjugated sex,' as they are called, have an
immensely better opportunity for study and intellectual progress than men — such superior opportunity,
indeed, that women, judging by this fact alone,
ought to occupy the foremost place in all the higher
intellectual fields of thought and effort. Literature,
madam, has given us Jane Austen, Miss Edgeworth,
Agnes Strickland, Mrs. Hemans, Charlotte Brontë,
Mrs. Somerville, George Eliot, George Sand, Mrs.
Oliphant, Jean Ingelow, Mrs. Stowe, and a host of
other admirable female writers; in art, there have

been Angelica Kaufmann, Rosa Bonheur, and recently a whole array of capable women-workers; Sid-
dons, O'Neil, Ellen Tree, Rachel, Ristori, Cushman,
have adorned the dramatic art; Malibran, Sontag,
Jenny Lind, Alboni, Patti, Nilsson, and many others,
have been a charm on the lyric stage; in truth, the
intellectual and art branches of human effort fairly
glitter with the names of women whose 'intellectual
activity' quietly sought out the fields for which their
genius fitted them, and in those fields speedily acquired 'name and fame.' It is, therefore, entirely
obvious that women may be as intellectual as their
capabilities will permit, without their mingling with
the wrangles of the legislative chamber, usurping
the places of the judges on the bench, or devoting
themselves to the high art of the suffrage. But let
me say that, while women are clamoring for greater
liberty in their intellectual activities, men at the
same time are bitterly complaining of the indifference
of women to all subjects of political, scientific, or
practical concern. If in our social intercourse we
found women abounding with intellectual force, ex-
hausting the opportunities at their command, over-
flowing the bounds that restrict them with their
surplus energy, we might well then be eager to make
room for them in the courts, or at Washington, and
elsewhere; but, as society stands, it is obvious enough

that women can find plenty of things at hand for the exercise of their 'intellectual activities' without our remaking the laws of Nature or upheaving the foundations of society.

—— " *Would I give woman education?*   Madam, true education was never given to any one ; people are never taught ; they only learn.   The education that a person possesses depends upon his capacity for taking possession of ideas and facts, his power of appropriation, his faculty for fusing crude ore and making it fine metal.   Things that are *taught* pass through the mind as water runs through a basket ; things that a man of his own force *learns* become part of himself.   Do not imagine for a moment that academies and colleges simply of themselves make education possible ; it has been shrewdly said that a man can be a fool in seven languages. Education is possible only where there is an active, absorbing, analyzing, searching mind—and this mind always becomes learned wherever it is.   Read the lives of those wonderful self-taught Scotch naturalists and geologists, Edward and Dick, and never say a word more about woman's deficiency of opportunity.

    "And let it not, madam, be perpetually assumed that education simply means the acquisition of learning, or the mastery of a mass of facts. It is not so much mere culture that is required for women as character — that sort of training that gives to the mind largeness, health, repose, and solidity of understanding. We have all met highly cultivated women who have been unstable of character and weak in judgment; brilliant, but vain, frivolous, and irrational creatures; and very unfortunate for the world would it be if women of this type were to be substituted for the women of the people, who, often unlearned in books, have yet in the great school of life acquired fortitude, strength, sobriety, and earnestness. The highest attribute of woman, after virtue and modesty, is character. If we could so educate our women that the nobler conditions of their nature would expand — if they could acquire in schools profound sincerity of feeling, large judgment, intellectual discernment and balance, we might well be indifferent to the exact extent of their purely literary acquisitions. There is, of course, no reason why learning and high culture should not only accompany these virtues, but really enforce and strengthen them; unless, indeed, they do so, their real value is open to dispute; but do not all the facts around us show that a fairly superstitious reverence prevails as to the saving grace of mere knowledge—of familiarity with books and a taste for art? Education seems to

mean with many a mere cataloguing of facts. The
man or woman who has studied at college or from
a printed page is supposed to be entitled to higher
credit than one who has acquired his facts at first
hand—by the study of nature or the observation of
men; and one who has a smattering of all the arts
is assumed to stand on a higher plane than another
who has learned wisdom by the right use of judgment. First of all, madam, let education, physical
and mental, make our girls large - natured women
—women robust in *physique* and robust in mind,
charged with high sentiment, capable of giving to
the world men formed after their own noble mold;
and then the refinements of culture would come as
graceful embroidery to the substantial fiber.

——"*Are not men and women equal?* The sum of
two different things may be equal, but unlike things,
madam, are never alike, despite all the female philosophers in the universe; and the unlikeness between men and women established by Nature can
never be abolished by conventions, platforms, or statutes. Every race, every nation, every period, every
community, every class, every profession, has its distinctive characteristics, and hence it is tolerably certain that each sex has its specific qualities. Now,
one quality of the masculine intellect is the power

of abstraction. It has the faculty of dealing with things upon the pure basis of abstract fact. But the female intellect deals with things in relation to persons only. Its approach to analysis is always through its sympathies; and this peculiarity of woman's constitution is indisputably radical, inasmuch as it springs from her instincts of maternity. To say that a nature charged through and through with the great divinity of motherhood has mental likeness to a sex unmoved by this great power, is to abolish all conditions of distinction, and to form conclusions regardless of testimony to the contrary. The whole range of woman's nature, madam, is toned and colored by this one supreme fact of her composition. It limits her range of speculation by concentrating her power of affection; it withdraws her sympathies from what is remote to what is personal and near; it establishes a relation with things of the world almost exclusively through her affections. What she is not inspired to love, she has no inspiration to heed. Within her pulse beats the pulse of mankind. All the facts and speculations in the world become subordinated to the powerful longings and sympathies this great link with the race establishes. Hence the essential necessity for mental activity in woman is, that her development should be through her affinities. She can not be abstract; she must be personal. In lit-

tle things and big things this is apparent. Woman
has a passion for novel-reading, because her sympathies are so keen; and she makes the best of novel-
writers, because she feels so quickly the pulse of
passion. The very gossip that a woman delights in
is one consequence of her absorption of the personality of people. She is nothing, except in contact with her kind. She likes society better than
men do, and solitude less. She lives almost solely
in her relations to the human family. All this being
true, it is evident that her mental culture should
have its own distinct aims. It is not necessary for
any practical end that it should be the same as
men's, and it can only produce good fruit by being
consonant to the law of her nature. If a woman
knew no Greek nor Latin, no mathematics nor philosophy, but surrendered her imagination to the
great masters of literature; if poetry, music, and
art, filled her soul with their mellowing touches; if
the forests and fields revealed their secrets of beauty to her; if her mind became thus enriched with
the most sympathetic facts in literature and nature,
we should discover in her some of the happiest and
most edifying aspects of culture. As men's muscles
do the severer manual labor, let their brains perform
the severer mental labor. In women there should be
that development which gives the largest grace of

womanhood, and the supremest culture in the arts that humanize and adorn.

"*Your lives are vapid and purposeless!* Are they to be rendered purposeful in any right sense by plunging into the discords of life? Need they be vapid and purposeless, with all the sciences and all literature and all nature before you? Make an object in life, by all means, and do not imagine that this is only possible by having the unattainable brought to your door, or by a fiat that translates you into men; for we, too, are full of similar discontents, we, too, are too often ignorant of the art of living—an art, madam, that consists in the knowledge of how to be interested in the things that lie in our daily paths—in the art of seizing and appropriating things, of putting our heart and intellect into relation with the facts of life and the phenomena of nature, and this is better than ambition, or the hurly-burly of life. Ambition is an appetite that grows upon what it feeds. Discontent more often eats into the heart of the successful man than into that of the humble one. Women who escape from the dominion of the hearth-stone into the broad field of struggle and triumph are not going thereby to conquer or silence their spirit of unrest — that

'. . . fever at the core,
Fatal to him who bears, to all who ever bore.'

Those who fret to-day over their vapid and purposeless lives may come in some future day to fret
over their successes, longing for new worlds to conquer.   Discontent was never yet, since the world
began, allayed by the acquisitions of ambition.   Your
remedy lies solely in intellectual occupation and pursuits, which are as free to you, as I have already
said, as to men.

"And let me say that the best gifts in the
world are those of seeing and hearing.   A great
many people have eyes, but very few have eye-
sight.   A great many have senses and faculties, but
very few know how to fully employ them.   Man or
woman endowed with the usual gifts of sight, and
observation, and mental force, must have discovered
some effective way of paralyzing and suppressing
them, if he or she travels down the years a purposeless life.   There are hundreds of things around the
most humble and circumscribed life that are capable of giving it purpose, and supplying it with zest.
The book of Nature is open to woman, with her
fine susceptibilities more completely so than to men;
and here are exhaustless things of interest.   Every
woman may become so much of an artist, at least,

as to learn to enjoy form and color—enough of an artist to open her eyes and note the endless charms which a devoted and intelligent spirit can see in the woods, the rocks, the sea, and the skies. Every woman may become enough of a botanist, entirely · by her own exertions, to find a hundred significant facts and delights in the plants that she now treads recklessly under her feet. Every woman may be enough of a geologist or a naturalist to learn from the stones pleasing lessons, and to find in animal life endless facts of the profoundest interest. Now and then a woman may make a discovery in one of these pursuits, and so win fame ; but not for fame, not for what the world may say, not for the gratification of vanity, but purely for the sake of themselves, must these studies be pursued if they are to effectually silence the spirit of unrest.

—— " *Men would make of women household drudges !* Madam, what fair and right-minded men ask of women is that they should fill a place which has certain definite boundaries, but one not less in character than that enjoyed by the other sex, al-though differing from it. It would be a great thing for the happiness of mankind, madam, if women could form adequately that necessary complement to the other sex by which its deficient conditions would be supplied—giving to the intercourse of two opposites the fullness of one complete existence; contrasting against the struggle and warfare of man the repose and meditative calm of woman, against the harsh and rugged aspects of competitive employment the ripe culture and æsthetic taste of an imagination permitted to expand in an atmosphere housed in from care and struggle. One may sometimes indulge in ideal pictures of life; and my ideal of men and women in their associated lives depicts the woman full of large and serene sympathy, capable of thinking upon all subjects of human concern, but as specially kindling in the members of the household an appreciation of the beautiful in all its many forms of art, music, poetry, and conduct. Why, when so many different things are to be done in the world, is it that women insist upon doing those things that the masculine sex can do so much better, and avoiding those more admirable things which women only can do well? If our strong-minded pleaders could fully understand how complete and perfect their happiness might be on the æsthetic and imaginative side of life, they would scarcely seek to mingle in the harsh competitions of the world, which they can not touch without losing those characteristics which all ages and all peoples have united in desiring for women—without substi-

tuting acuteness for meditation, sharpness for soft-
ness, contention for calm, noise and bustle for taste
and sympathy, warfare for peace. A world in which
all the women simply copied and echoed all the
men, in which a man found in the wife of his
bosom a rival in his profession, where the contest
and struggle of life were repeated at the hearth-
stone, would prove a dreadful weariness to the body
and the spirit. The millennium, madam, does not
lie in that direction. In the name of all that is
desirable, I beg certain declaimers to try and understand a few elementary principles—to realize that
everything under heaven is a law to itself, and that
nothing whatsoever can successfully fill the place or
live the life of any other distinct thing. The felicity of human association depends upon the acceptance of just this principle—of perceiving the relation
of parts, the division of duties and privileges, and
upon recognizing that the perfection of the whole is
attainable only by the due subordination of the several parts. The world will get along much better
with first-rate men-men, and first-rate women-women,
than by confounding the qualities of the two, and
giving us very inferior masculine women and worthless feminine men.

" There is no danger that women will be unsexed

by enlarging their sphere of activity! This depends, madam, upon the nature of the enlargement of this sphere. It certainly will not unsex women to enlarge their activity in study; they may know a great deal more than they do now about history, and philosophy, and science, and literature, and art, without any loss to their womanliness; but if 'enlarging their sphere of activity' means making politicians of them, sending them to Congress, making lawyers and judges of them, then I beg to say that under this experience they would most decidedly become unsexed. Can the qualities of any thing— of any human, any animal, or any plant even—remain unchanged with all its environments altered? It is impossible in nature that new conditions should not cause a fresh adaptation and adjustment. If men and women are to receive the same education, attempt the same professions, experience the same contentions, undergo the same struggles, be trained in the same facts, and crammed with the same ideas —to be in all their contact with the world the same entities, as it were — it is simply impossible that all the distinction of feeling, and taste, and principle, that now exists, should remain unchanged. A man may not care whether such a change occurs or not, but if he *does* care, if he thinks that a man-woman is not an estimable or an agreeable thing for the contemplation of gods or men, then let him have the wit to see that the womanliness of woman can only be preserved by her isolation from the ruder phases of life, by that feminine culture and training under which her tastes and her faculties are rightly developed. Let us have robust, stalwart, hard-headed men, and let us have lovable and delightful women; let all the qualities that make great masculine natures be assiduously cultivated, and all the qualities that make gentle women be also assiduously cultivated, but with no confusion whatever as to their characteristics, duties, and tasks. Those people who like the sexes mixed can do something toward accomplishing their purpose, but they will have to encounter two formidable obstacles—nature being one, and the honest instincts of the great multitude of men and women being the other.

—— "*Men are afraid of learned and brilliant women!* Madam, the men thus charged with mental pusillanimity in regard to intellectual women are not commonly supposed to exhibit a similar dread of learned and accomplished persons of their own sex. No man withholds from a club because great men belong to it. No man is afraid of a career at the bar, in literature, or in politics, because distinguished persons are connected with those profes-

sions, whom it will probably be his destiny to meet
and perhaps professionally to encounter. Men, if
anything, are over-confident in all intellectual struggles with their fellows; self-respect, or pride, or conceit—some motive either worthy or unworthy—pre-
vents them from acknowledging inferiority, even if
they are conscious of it. It can not, therefore, be
that men dislike learned women because they are
apprehensive of intellectual fence. People are usually too unconscious of defeat in all encounters of
wit to dread it much. Their very insensibility to
the palpable hits and the verbal triumphs of an op-
ponent give them no fear of the conversational
arena. The dullness or the indifference of men in
this particular is alone, madam, sufficient to prevent
them from disliking ability in women; and then
every man is so profoundly assured of the intellectual inferiority of your sex that, in the abundance
of his confidence, he has no doubt. Clever men
know that the most brilliant women are always vul-
nerable in argument, and stupid men talk on without ever knowing they are defeated.

" *Why, then, is conspicuous ability disliked in wom-
en ?* Are you not assuming your ground ? Is it
certain that men are offended at the evidence of
talent in your sex? Yet in a certain form it must

be conceded they are. Every man imagines women
of genius in whom he could find delight; but, whatever learned women may say or think about the
matter, the first, the second, and the third essential
quality that every man admires in his mother or
seeks for in a wife is womanliness. If genius and
learning can enhance this supreme grace, genius and
learning will be admired in women; but, so long as
it is believed that intellectual force extinguishes or
diminishes delicacy, gentleness, and sweetness, men
will dread its manifestation in their wives and daughters. Frivolity and insipidity, which men are ac-
cused of liking in women, are simply accepted with
forbearance when they are accompanied by those
charms of sex that make women delightful, and
which compensate for so many shortcomings. Judgment, taste, discretion, vivacity—all good qualities
of sound minds, are excellent things; but even these
in women must be fused into a harmonious, mellow,
unobtrusive unity. Delicacy of apprehension, quick-
ness of perception, capacity of appreciation—these
supreme womanly qualities of mind every man of
taste, I assure you, delights in; but loud argument,
boisterous assertion, clamorous talk, these things men
do most decidedly dread in women, and these things
have too commonly marked our intellectual Amazons.
Do not, madam, let women lay the flattering unc-

tion to their souls that men fear their mental superiority; let them rather believe that there is gallantry enough among us yet even to delight in their victories over ourselves ; but let them understand that, so long as man inherits the nature of Adam, the primal delight of his heart will be in fresh, fair, and gentle women, and every honest man will confess that he does fear in woman whatever may tend to rob her of these graces. Perhaps you think all this very commonplace. Well, so I fear it is— it is so true and common that it has been known since the world began."

IX

MR. BLUFF ON MODERN FICTION.

(In the Library.)

BACHELOR BLUFF,
A CRITIC.

Bluff. There is no greater blunder, sir, than to assume that stories which depict the throes of heated passion or the perturbations of well-bred lovers in a drawing-room are of a higher intellectual rank than narratives of adventure and exploit.

Critic. How can you say this? Assuredly analysis of character is the highest and most subtile phase of the novelist's art.

Bluff. High and subtile, I grant, but it has not the whole field. There are not only other worthy things than the study of emotions and motives, but psychological probing, when pushed too far, is apt to become a great bore, and not unfrequently stimulates an unhealthful and morbid passion for introspection. It is not a good thing, sir, to be always looking into our own minds or into the minds of our neighbors. The subjective novel within due limits is proper enough to read and study, but when made too large a part of our intellectual food the result is morally and mentally hurtful. The breezy, out-of-door, objective novel affords an excellent counter-current of sensation, and for this reason alone it ought to be sandwiched between the highly seasoned preparations of the subjective school.

Critic. But peculiarities of mind, tendencies of feeling, and operation of motive are necessary to give vitality to character. Without them the people of a story would not seem to be genuine, and consequently would fail to awaken the reader's sympathies. It requires the highest order of skill to depict character truthfully and logically; to look into the minds of men and see their workings, to trace the operations of cause and effect, and to measure accurately and depict authentically the reflex actions of temperament and emotion.

Bluff. No doubt; and it requires the highest order of skill to be a great surgeon, but what have you and I to do with anatomy? What business have healthful minds to be probing among the diseases of the body or the mind? It is not disease but health that should attract healthful men, and those works of art that depict the bright, the felicitous, the open, the robust, are the most useful to mankind, whether the skill required for them be more or less. The reasons that make us like epic poems, that lead us to admire the temples and statues of the ancients, that give to form and color so much fascination, are the elementary foundations of the objective novel. If it is a fine thing to be sensitive to the beauties of nature, it must be a fine thing to be sensitive to pictures of life that are closely related to those open aspects of the world around us; and, if architecture stands high in the æsthetic world, if color in painting is entitled to our admiration, if the lines of sculpture are worthy of our study, then romances which deal preëminently with color and form are candidates for an equal appreciation. The novel of action is an epic in prose; the novel of picturesque situation is like a stirring painting on canvas; and the novel that gives us heroes and heroines of ideal grace and beauty awakens in us some of the same sensations that higher sculpture does. The arts generally deal with the objective, appealing exclusively to the senses; and it is therefore certainly not a feeble or unworthy thing for the novelist to appeal to the same sensibilities that painters and sculptors do. It is only by realizing the really high place in art that novels of description and action may occupy when the performance is equal to the plan, that one is prepared to form a just estimate of romances like Scott's and Cooper's.

Critic. But, assuredly, you place these novels much below George Eliot's?

Bluff. Do I place Greek literature below your modern would-be psychological romance? Do I place the greatest of your psychological heroines below Shakespeare's Rosalind or Portia? Is the Apollo Belvedere a lesser work of art than George Eliot's Gwendolen? I must not compare things so different, you say, but comparisons of distinctly different things sometimes bring us up sharply and enable us to see where we are. The art and literature of the past which the world could least afford to lose are almost wholly objective—works that deal with the external, with beauty, action, courage, and force. Shall I tell you what I consider the most perfect figure in our American literature? It is young Uncas, in Cooper's " Last of the Mohicans." He incarnates the three special qualities of the hero —youth, grace, and daring; and neither Hector, nor Paris, nor Perseus has greater fascinations than that strange and almost mystic figure would have possessed had he also come down to us from the remote past. As a product of Greek imagination he would have embodied the melancholy, the beauty, and the spirit of the woods, just as the German sprite Undine does of the waters. He would have figured in endless statues and paintings, and have fired the fancy of innumerable poets. But, born close to us, being our very own, we have lacked the faculty of seeing in him the exquisite poetical conditions that three thousand years ago would have made him immortal. We think we appreciate the heroes of Greek story because we have been industriously instructed how to admire them, but we have shown an utter lack of ability to seize for ourselves upon a singularly beautiful figure of our own land and time, which as a type of a splendid young savage is unique and artistically perfect. He is filled with the very breath of poetry, and yet neither our painters, our poets, nor our sculptors have discovered him. It may some day be thought that this Adonis of the woods is as worthy of attention as diseased studies in spiritual anatomy, and we may be sure that our tastes will not be healthful, robust, strong, or sweet until this time comes about.

Critic. I am really astonished at your selection of this figure as your ideal of a creation in art. I should certainly have expected rather a selection from Hawthorne, if an American author must be preferred.

Bluff. Oh! I read Hawthorne with immense interest, but can you believe that his creations, fascinating as they are, can possibly influence the mind as wholesomely as Cooper's young savage? Health is always out-of-doors; in the air, and the breeze, with open, transparent life. All the world is continually talking about the philosophic Hamlet, and measuring Shakespeare's power by this character and his Macbeth and Othello; but, sir, to my mind that in which Shakespeare conspicuously asserts his superiority, in which he transcends everything else in imaginative literature, is his female characters—his Rosalind, Portia, Imogen, Viola, Miranda, Beatrice, Juliet, Isabella, Desdemona, Ophelia. Here we have a superb and wonderful sisterhood unmatched anywhere, and fairly unmatchable. By these women Shakespeare separates himself distinctly from every other dramatist and novelist; nowhere else are wit, vivacity, beauty, purity of feeling, womanliness, elevation of character, and a superb poetic gayety, so admirably and exquisitely blended as in Rosalind, Portia, and Viola. If you should place on one side all the other creatures of the imagination in English literature and on the other side the women of Shakespeare, and force me to choose between them, I would take Rosalind and her sisterhood, and let the rest go. There is no spiritual anatomy nor psychological dissection in a line that Shakespeare

wrote about them. They are glorious by the standard of the most perfect art—because they penetrate
with delight, because they elevate the imagination,
because they charm the fancy, because they excite
the profoundest and purest pleasure.

Critic. Tell me what you consider the purpose
of fiction.

Bluff. The current notion appears to be that the
end of fiction is to depict the mishaps and defeats
of life with realistic fidelity. The heroes and heroines of the earlier novel underwent innumerable
tribulations, but always in the end overcame adverse
circumstances as well as enemies, and sat down in
peace with their hearts' desires accomplished. This
regulation *dénoûment* is now unfashionable, and story-
writers absolutely take excessive pains to make their
characters permanently unhappy. A marriage in the
last chapter is looked upon as a weak concession to
a conventional and inartistic prejudice, and heroes
and heroines are consequently made for the express
purpose of exemplifying defeat, and showing how the
best-laid plans may come to grief. It seems to be
the accepted method to select characters with marked
flaws in them, in order to indicate how "the rift"
will "by-and-by make the music mute." This wan-
ton design to make sadness the fashion clearly arises
from the notion that art should consist of devices

7

for showing all the unhandsome features of life, all
the disagreeable and calamitous possibilities that beset mankind; and he is thought to be a master-hand
who is most expert in multiplying mischances, and
who exhibits the greatest ingenuity in bringing right
things to wrong ends. Now, sir, the real reason for
the novel, the why and wherefore that men and
women delight in the fictitious fortunes of other men
and women, is because something is given which
supplements nature, which bestows that which life
too often denies. Every man has at heart a passionate love for what I will call the symmetries of
fate—for the rewards that follow earnest and honest
endeavor, and the justice that gives us finally full
compensation for all that we endure. Through all
the calamities and mishaps that surround us, we all
of us dream of possibilities—of the good that will
come by-and-by to cheer us; of difficulties assailed
and overcome, of enemies put down, of the felicitous
completion of our schemes. And it is exactly because these dreams so rarely come true in real life,
that people delight in those inventions called novels,
wherein wrong and suffering are or ought to be suit-
ably rectified. When mischance pursues us, there is
a delightful compensation in following the career of
a hero who overcomes misfortunes, and wrests things
to his own ends. In real life, bitterness and jeal-

ousy may be felt at the better fortunes of other
men ; but in the novel the hero is our very self, and
all his achievements and successes are enjoyed with
almost as much zest as if they were our very own.
The very foundation of fiction, sir, its significance
and meaning to most people, lie in this power to
reflect each reader in one of the principal person-
ages. It shows us what we would like to do, and
what we know we feel. The young lady who reads
many novels has many lovers, and is married many
times. Your psychological novel is valuable for this
reason solely, because it analyzes successfully our
own moods and emotions. The extent to which one
delights in the novel always depends upon the facility with which he can transfer himself in imagination to the pages he is reading. If fiction did not
succeed in getting us out of ourselves, in creating
worlds more delightful than the world we experience, in fashioning things better to our liking than
Fate fashions them, it is certain that novels would
go generally unread. The true function of the novel
is here apparent. It must give us pictures of life
with a great core of sweetness, enlarging our individuality by multiplying our experiences and delights
—the artistic requirements being simply that the
people and incidents shall be possible and wholly
thinkable. The writers who imagine they can se-

cure sympathy by endowing their characters with unheard-of virtues, or showering upon them impossible good fortunes, defeat their ends; but writers who, in disgust at these excesses, turn around and portray characters without charm, and substitute calamities for blessings, drift altogether away, not only from popular sympathy, but from the real purpose of the novel. Distinctly, nobody wants novels that reproduce all the sufferings and struggles of real life unless supplemented with those compensations that in real life ought to follow, but rarely do; for the novel is nothing more than a device for setting the disorders of life right, and making us all happy by the contemplation of final—and so often rightly called poetic—justice. The novel that does not do this thing may entertain a good many people by its character-sketches and its descriptions, but, in missing the fundamental purpose of fiction, must fail to command the sympathies of the great world of readers.

Critic. The rude and stirring novels of Mesdames Holmes and Southworth, that have such a hold in certain rural sections, must, according to your rule, be the very best of novels — for they accomplish effectually for their readers all that you set down as the true purpose of fiction.

Bluff. Would they have their multitude of readers if they did not do this very thing? I dare say they have endless faults, but they would find no readers if they did not bring home to people some sweetness and pleasure. The only difference between these novels and better ones is, that the latter attempt to accomplish the same end with truer pictures of life and a higher literary quality—and often lose the end, let me say, by doing so.

Critic. A French critic declares that the quality conspicuously deficient in American fiction is *taste*. Unfortunately, this defect is strikingly characteristic in the works of the more popular of our writers. The American story-tellers who cultivate taste, who exhibit fastidiousness and artistic finish, are commonly without large constituencies of readers. And yet, singularly enough, English novelists of the first class are very widely read in America.

Bluff. Then it is evident that native authors of superior culture are not neglected because they aim too high. A public that devours tens of thousands of a novel by George Eliot, or William Black, or Thomas Hardy, shows its capacity to rise to the level of the most fastidious of our own writers of fiction. The difficulty is, that our own authors imagine that fastidiousness means the exclusion of sympathy and passion. Literary folk and certain people who always take a place by the side of literary leaders whether they understand or not, have great admiration for two or three Boston story-writers, and measure other people's culture by their estimate of those writers' books.   They are very good books indeed, very noticeable for keen insight into character and for refined subtilty, but refinement and subtilty are never enough of themselves to command a wide suffrage. The mountain-stream is clear, sparkling, and full of beauty, but it is the broad, deep sea that encompasses.   Of pleasant and sparkling literary rivulets we have enough; we all long for the majesty and power of the deep—for books that shall have finish and taste without losing the pulse of humanity, that shall stir our passions and our sympathies profoundly without transcending the bounds of nature or the laws of art.   Our better writers seem to be frightened at the turbulence of actual life and the passions of earnest men and women; they play on the verge of the great expanses of life, dallying with trifles, analyzing queer specimens, asking us to admire them because they have dissected a blade of grass, and lamenting because the world casts but a half-glance at their pretty toys.   It is simply impossible that these writers should find acceptance with the general public.   There are English novelists that have all their refinement with a large measure of real power, with strong sympathies, with deeper currents of feeling, and these writers must inevitably be preferred to our own writers so long as the latter prefer intellectual legerdemain to earnest purpose, and are content to address their tasteful nothings to each other and their little parlor circles rather than write for the great world at large.

Critic. In asserting that the purpose of fiction is to adjust what you call the "symmetry of fate," you overlook the significant fact that those works of imagination which have a tragical termination have always had a deeper and more lasting hold upon the world than any other. And the same thing exists in historic passages. Who would care for the story of Hero and Leander had those young people's love-adventure ended in marriage? It is the sad fate of Juliet and Francesca that makes their stories so well remembered. Beatrice Cenci would have long since been forgotten had her career ended happily. It is the dismal fate of Mary Queen of Scots that makes her story the most read of any queen in history. When Dickens brought Little Nell to an early grave, he took the surest method of immortalizing her.

Bluff. People always remember pains longer than pleasure. A shock of any kind is never forgotten, but this scarcely proves that the shock was agreeable, or that it is right to inflict gratuitous suffering.

Then, again, the immortality which ill-fated heroes and heroines experience is partly due to the perpetual protest against the deep damnation of their taking-off.

Critic. I think it is due to the fact that sympathy and grief are more profound than pleasure.

Bluff. I wonder who would care for the fates of imaginative heroes and heroines if they were not lovers? Love is the passion, my good sir, that makes the whole world kin. Youth and beauty and love prematurely perishing—the thought is so exquisitely painful, so penetrating and intense, that the whole nature rises up in rebellion against the idea. For this reason catastrophes of this kind are only permissible in high-wrought poems, dealing with well-known tragedies. No man should invent a tragedy, and especially a tragedy of life of to-day. There has been and is too much suffering in the world to make such a thing endurable. The novel, moreover, is a picture of life, of character, of manners ; it is a comedy; it is an insight into modes of feeling and action ; it is a revelation of familiar phases of existence; and tragedy is too lofty and intense for the canvas. Let one take the story of Hero and Leander, or of Francesca, or of Juliet, and weave it into a poem, if he will, thereby simply emphasizing a sad story already known, but to my mind tragedy needs historic perspective, the mist of distance, the sense that it is irretrievable, to commend it to my sympathies.

Critic. Sympathy seems to me the one universal gift of mankind ; it is not limited to class or period.

Bluff. Oh, everybody knows how to weep, but it takes a fine texture of mind to know thoroughly how to enjoy the bright and happy things of life.

Critic. The easiest thing in the world is to move people to laughter.

Bluff. By buffoonery, yes. Antics will always set an audience in the theatre in a roar, when lightness, brilliancy, wit, the flash and sparkle of genuine gayety, are scarcely felt at all. Gayety, let me tell you, is the rarest thing in literature ; and it is the most difficult thing an actor is called upon to express— so difficult, indeed, that we now rarely find it on the stage at all. A rude throng blubbers at sentiment and roars at buffoonery ; it is only the best minds that delight in intellectual grace, in fine thoughts finely expressed, in the happy phrase, in the winning word, in the Saladin blade of comedy.

Critic. Does not a delight in mere brilliancy, in gay lightness, indicate a moral deficiency ? People whose moral sense is acute can not fail to take a serious view of life, perhaps even a sad one, and to those minds vivacity always appears thoughtless and heartless.

Bluff. Vivacity is not a product of psychological study, no doubt.   It is another form of objective art; it is a part of the splendor of the external; it is a form of paganism.   Have you ever thought, by-the-way, of the extent to which paganism characterizes our fiction.   The utter exclusion of every form of religious belief or sentiment from many novels wide-ly read by the best classes is very surprising and per-haps significant.   These novels are not irreligious; they are simply non-religious.   They are not hostile to religion in any of its forms; they do not deny the validity of faith, nor oppose, either directly or by implication, any of the creeds or any current dogma; they simply are as silent in regard to relig-ion as if there were no such thing in the world. They are not more completely insensible to condi-tions of mind and thought that may be supposed to exist in Jupiter or Venus than they are dumb to the profoundest and the most prevailing phases of feeling that exist.   I have no great liking for the specially religious novel, in which there is often an offensive intrusion of pious sentiment; but that any one should undertake to portray conflicts of passion and emotion, to give what are designed to be faith-ful delineations of life, and yet ignore currents of thought and motives of action which enter into and radically color all phases of human existence and human experience, is really very extraordinary. I have just been reading Black's "Macleod of Dare," and found myself in contact with people utterly without the religious instinct — who, oppressed by sorrows, suffering under misfortunes, thwarted in their hopes, plunged into grief and despair, exhibit not the slightest perception of a great Christian scheme which is specially designed to bring solace to the heavy-hearted and offer compensation in the future for sufferings endured here. Neither the grief-stricken mother and her attendants in Castle Dare, nor the gay pleasure-seekers in the heart of fashionable London, seem ever to have heard of such a thing as an overruling Providence, of such a trust as faith, of such a duty as submission, of such a promise as immortality, of such a possession as Christianity. This utter exclusion of religious thought I have named paganism, but even the pagans called upon their gods, and had vague surmises as to worlds beyond this, while these men and women are as insensible to every religious aspiration as so many statues. Now, the question is, was this elimination of Christianity conscious or unconscious—a deliberate purpose to cast out God, or simply an evasion of an idea that would have uncomfortably complicated the artistic design of the author? The latter is probably the true solution, yet how is it that re-

ligious convictions should thus complicate the purpose of a writer? And how, assuming it to be true,
is he privileged to disregard an important factor in
his problem simply because it adds to his difficulties? Black, as we all know, is skillful and tireless
in his analysis of motive and feeling; he penetrates
the workings of the heart, and attempts to reveal all
its mysteries, yet he deliberately eliminates a whole
range of emotions, casts out a definite and powerful
body of influences. Whether he is a believer or not
makes no difference. Whatever his own religious convictions may be, he was bound, I affirm, in depicting
his imaginary people, to show them governed by the
ideas and living under the conditions that pertain
to men and women in real life. I am citing Mr.
Black simply as a representative of the modern sec-
ular novelist. In numerous other novels a similar
paganism is evinced. Now, it is right enough, artistically, for novelists to depict their heroes and
heroines as rejecting Christianity; they may imagine
at pleasure communities of infidels and pagans, and
they may trace the growth of a man's heart and
mind who has been educated in entire neglect of
religion; but how can they be justified in portray-
ing characters who, being reared in the midst of
Christian influences, yet act as if there were no such
thing as Christianity? I ask this question more in

the interest of art than of morals. I do not think it at all certain that novels would be chastened or their influence rendered better by the incorporation of religious sentiment—which may so readily be caricatured or distorted. My argument simply is, that pictures of life can not be considered true or adequate that fail to measure the full sum of things that make up our civilization and go to form the average man and woman.

Critic. I agree with you here fully.

X

SOME OF MR. BLUFF'S POLITICAL NOTIONS.

(On the Train.)

BACHELOR BLUFF,
A POLITICIAN.

"A GREAT statesman," exclaimed Mr. Bluff, "is only a great negation." This was said in reply to a comment of his traveling companion, a distinguished politician.

"Nothing more," retorted the politician, in a tone and with a smile of mild derision. Mr. Bluff caught the intonation and saw the smile. He gathered himself together at once, and replied with animation:

"Yes, a great negation, sir, and nothing else. His duty is simply to stand sentinel over the interests of society in order to protect them from the presumptuous intermeddling of fools."

"Undoubtedly," said the politician, "he must

guard the interests of society, but that is a poor general who always remains on the defensive. Your statesman must advance; he must originate; he must organize rightful forces as well as restrain dangerous ones."

"Do not," said the Bachelor, "reason by analogy. That is always misleading. What is required of generals is no criterion of what is required of statesmen. In society there are immense natural forces at work, which regulate affairs when left to their undisturbed operation far better than the wisest men that ever lived could do. Were it possible for a man to arise who could comprehend all the intricate workings of society, who could follow through all their mazes the operations of the innumerable threads that make up the complex web of life, we should have a statesman to whom we might gladly entrust the organization and direction of affairs; but such a man, sir, would be too wise to thrust his hand into the complex social machinery. He might be able to see where a clog arrested the free action of the parts, where this or that thread met with obstructions, and by removing these extraneous things promote the general ease and smoothness of the movement—and this is all."

"You believe, then, in a sort of government by nature—an adjustment of the whole complicated in-

terests of society by two or three primary principles.
Your notions, sir, would work, perhaps, in elementary conditions of society, but it needs, in an advanced civilization, the supremest knowledge and
highest skill to stand at the helm and successfully
pilot the bark of state."

"There is no such knowledge and no such skill,"
interrupted Mr. Bluff. "They have never been mani-
fested. They have never been displayed, even by
your greatest men."

"Never, sir?"

"Never! It is true there has grown up in the
course of centuries a code of laws, written and un-
written, which embody altogether a great deal of
political wisdom — but this wisdom is almost wholly
of a negative character. It has taken thousands of
years for legislatures and courts of justice to discover with some show of knowledge what men *shall
not* and *must not* do; but all the wise men of the
world have not been able to wisely determine what
men *shall do*—excepting, perhaps, the single thing,
that they must render justice, that they must respect
the rights and property of others. And yet all this
is distinctly negative. Thou shalt not steal! Thou
shalt not murder! Thou shalt not bear false witness! Thou shalt not commit adultery! Here we
have all the law, and all that courts and legislatures

can rightly do is to compel their observance, or pun-
ish their violation—that is, to create and maintain a
thorough police. All other governmental direction
of affairs can do nothing but work mischief; indeed,
all other forms of governmental interference *have* done
nothing but work mischief."

" Nothing," said the politician, with smiling com-
posure—"nothing but one vast, impassive, sublime
negation ! No reforms for the innumerable evils of
our social organizations, no plans for the education
and intellectual development of the people, no
thought of moral duties and spiritual life, no attempt to advance the race to higher planes of civilization."

" By Jove, sir," roared the Bachelor, "you have
the whole transcendental programme pat ! Who for a
moment wishes to deter the advancement of civilization, and all that ? I am talking about the duties of government, not the duties of the Church, or
the college, or the Sunday-school—of those governmental duties which will enable the Church and the
college, and all other institutions, to work out their
purposes to the greatest and completest advantage.
There is perpetually this confusion between the voluntary social and religious forces of society and the
administration of government. The other day I
read in an essay by Froude, the historian, a passage

which, as I remember, ran as follows : 'A state of things in which the action of government is restricted to the prevention of crime and statutable fraud, and where beyond these things all men are left to go their own way—to be honest or dishonest, pure or profligate, wise or ignorant, to lead what lives they please and preach what doctrines they please —may have been a necessary step in the evolution of humanity; but, as surely, if no other principle had been ever heard of or acted on, civilization would have stood still, hardly above the level of barbarism.' "

"Upon my word, sir," interrupted the politician, "this seems to me very sound argument. Where would civilization be without the aid and guidance of a wise authority ? "

"Where, sir ? I do not know what *wise* authority would have done for us, but authority such as the world has experienced has rather held civilization by the throat. But what does Mr. Froude mean ? Now, it is true that a society or community in which no other principle had ever been heard of than that of the 'prevention of crime and statutable fraud,' where men were honest or dishonest, pure or profligate, wise or ignorant, as they chanced, 'would have stood still,' as Mr. Froude says, 'hardly above the level of barbarism.' But if this means that no community can rise above the level of barbarism where the *government* is actuated by no other principle than that of the prevention of crime and statutable fraud, then the argument, sir, is false through and through, from the foundation upward, and is false with such a curious inversion as to afford a remarkable illustration of how completely the records of the race can be misread. No community, obviously, can advance in civilization unless there are powerful moral and intellectual forces at work; but it so happens that the governments of the past, even the most paternal and the most illustrious, have commonly obstructed rather than aided those forces. Governments have very much neglected the prevention of crime, have rarely efficiently punished statutable frauds, and they have been commonly intensely indifferent to the honesty or dishonesty, the purity or the profligacy, the wisdom or the ignorance, of the people. They have, however, been very zealous in behalf of favorite ecclesiasticisms, and have endeavored with all their might to maintain certain forms of religious belief. They have concerned themselves a good deal about dogma, but very little about morals; they haven't cared a straw about the purity or profligacy of the community, but have looked well to see that the people have paid their tithes, and acknowledged the supremacy of the

established Church.   In pursuance of these purposes
they have at various times constituted a good many
statutable offenses which in equity were not offenses,
and these fictitious crimes have been punished with
abundant energy.   At times when highways swarmed
with banditti, when no one could venture abroad
without means of defense, when robbery and violence abounded, when neither life nor property was
safe because of the gross neglect and indifference of
the state, men and women were zealously burned,
and whipped, and imprisoned, for some defection in
the way of religious belief.   At times when roads
were so neglected that travel was laborious and difficult, and rivers were without bridges ; when on all
sides was needed energetic administration in directions that would advance the practical welfare of the
people, rulers always exhibited zeal enough and
found resources enough to build grand cathedrals
and fine palaces.   The whole history of government, I affirm, is a record of meddlesome and oppressive things done and necessary things left undone.
The state has always taxed trade, handicapped in-
dustry, vexatiously embarrassed commerce, suppressed
opinion, retarded the growth of knowledge, hin-
dered intellectual activity, and proved itself in numerous things a common nuisance.   It has always
so retarded civilization, either by its interferences

or its neglects, that advance has been rendered possible only by controlling and subordinating it, by virtually dethroning it, by compelling it to keep within or nearly within its proper province. Rulers have never understood that, by simply limiting the function of government to the preservation of order, they would more effectually than by any other means bring all the forces of society into full and free activity. In view of the wretched mistakes and appalling crimes governments have thus committed, it is amazing to see a man like Mr. Froude confound things in the way he does — wholly confusing the forces that underlie government with the restrictions that operate in the name of government. The more we study the past the more it becomes evident that, while government is indispensable up to a certain point, our civilization has advanced in spite of it rather than by its aid. Governments have created more disorders than they have suppressed; they have made dangerous classes by their oppression and injustice; and, while we are not yet far enough advanced to do without them altogether, it is important to keep them closely to their proper work. Let them preserve order and keep the peace. Art and letters and industrial energy will carry on civilization triumphantly without their aid or interference. These things, indeed, so far have flourished pretty nearly in direct ratio to the extent that government has let them alone. The most important task now before the world is the subordination of government, forcing it within a rigid limitation of its powers and its duties."

" It would be impossible," replied the politician, " to hold people together without governmental authority. We should see the strong subjugating the weak; security of life and property would be unknown."

" Everybody knows that a police force must exist somewhere—a power to restrain the unruly, to prevent disorder. But it is absurd to suppose that the balance and stability of society are maintained by power or force of any kind. The millions of people in New York are not kept in order by fifteen hundred policemen; this police is necessary to adjust the incidental frictions that occur, and to repress the dangerous tendencies of an unruly few. Order is maintained among the mass because their interests are on the side of order. Wherever they are not on the side of order, nothing but a military despotism can maintain peace or security of any kind. To repress the unruly and adjust incidental collisions are the purposes of state machinery, but these are the very things that your ideal government has for the most part neglected. Politicians have been too busy with the intrigues of courts, or occupied in the appropriation of spoils, to look very closely after the maintenance of order or the administration of justice, and have generally made one with the strong in their subjugation of the weak. The nations have been torn to pieces by the quarrels and contests of rulers, by their thirst for power, by their greed for wealth, by their furious jealousies; and now and then a king or statesman has won immense fame by simply *not* furthering these evils, by not proving himself a curse to the people he rules over. This is the best that can be said for any of them. Every principle of constitutional liberty, every accepted political theory upon which our welfare rests, has come from the people, been forced upon rulers after many rebellions. Statesmen have invented nothing and discovered nothing; have never comprehended the foundations of society, the operations of interests, or the action of social forces. Principles have been discovered by philosophers in their closets, never by men in power. Statesmen have sometimes adopted the principles of philosophers— as in the case of Peel taking up the free trade of Adam Smith—but nothing valuable to mankind has come from the rulers of mankind?"

" Absolutely nothing, sir?" said the politician.

" Absolutely nothing. The greatest political discovery ever made is the principle that government has no rightful authority over the religious faiths of its subjects. It is absolutely impossible to over-state the importance of this principle — which our ancestors were the first to discover—which deprives the state of a power that has wrought more ruin and brought more suffering than almost any one thing else. This was a great step toward the liber-ty, peace, and security of the subject, but it did not come from men in power, and it is a principle little understood throughout the world among those in authority even to-day. It was a great step; but it is only one step. The next thing to establish is that government has nothing whatever to do with trade or commerce, except to protect it — by " protect," meaning simply police protection, guaranteeing to each man the right to work out his purposes, so long as they are not injurious to the purposes of others, in his own way, secure, unmolested, undisturbed."

"Your fierce censure of governments," remarked the politician, " is simply a censure of the wrongs they have committed and the mistakes they have made. As, despite these wrongs and mistakes, the people have developed from rude barbarism to gen-eral intelligence and civilization, I must think that governments, as a whole, have not been so bad."

"Civilization, sir, has advanced mainly in spite

of government—that is, in spite of the restrictions, the burdens, and the oppressions of government as it has existed—for obviously no government at all would have been even worse than the hard master which has ruled in that name. It seems to me that this is a very important thing for the world to realize — and apparently a very difficult one, for everywhere we see people adhering tenaciously to the notion that the state can remedy everything, that all things can be made sweet and comfortable if only the right laws are passed and enforced. Emphatically we want right laws, but we want very few laws; what people really need is to see that they owe to themselves and to nothing else such progress as they have made, that their well-being is the outcome of natural forces permitted to act without obstruction, that society is held together by its own internal coherence, and not by artificial pressure, and that it develops by its own elementary forces, and not by the dictation or the authority of statutes or makers of statutes."

"All people should be taught to love and respect authority."

"They should be taught to respect rightful authority, and to hold fettered to the earth all other bonds. They should be taught to obey necessary laws, and to scatter to the winds all others."

8

" Will they not mistake, and scatter to the winds wise laws? "

" They would soon discover that order is necessary, and that laws must be maintained which preserve order, and that all others are monstrous impertinences. They will, I trust, in time discover that statecraft is not nearly so great a thing as it is supposed to be ; that the politician fills a place far transcending his importance. Now they most unduly exalt him. They hang upon his doings, discuss his theories and his projects, watch his movements, listen to his utterances, and gossip about his intrigues. Glance at things at Washington, and the relation of the press and of the whole public to the doings there! We see scores of correspondents transmitting to the journals in every section elaborate reports of idle personal squabbles in the Congressional chambers. We find ponderous sheets and almost endless books and pamphlets devoted to recording debates that, for the most part, relate to party discipline, to the distribution of spoils, or to contests for office. Who shall or shall not be collector of the revenues of New York, or who shall distribute the mails at Philadelphia — or some matter of similar import — is continually agitating the country from one end to the other. Issues of this character fill thousands of newspapers with rumors and discus-

sions, load the mails with correspondence and pam-
phlet - speeches, keep busy an army of telegraph -
reporters, and fix the attention of the whole nation
upon the actors in the senseless struggle. Is there
anything else in the world so full of noise and
sound, heat and agitation, in behalf of a matter so
utterly insignificant? From the assembling of Congress until its adjournment, all its doings are watched
with a public concern which, to the philosophical
observer, is supremely absurd. Rarely, indeed, do
the political doings at the Capitol involve issues of
any real importance. There is a little tinkering of
the tariff, and an immense gathering of representatives of all sorts of interests to secure the tinkering
to their special advantage; there is a vast crowd of
hungry office-seekers flowing into the lobbies of Congress and the antechambers of the departments;
there are *levées* and dinner-parties by the high officials; there are a great number of bills for the pro-
motion of private ends continually urged upon the
attention of the learned legislators; there are fierce
debates between wise leaders that agitate each political faction to its center; there are revelations
of frauds, and explanations that explain them away,
and more explanations that explain the explained;
there is an immense fund of gossip and scandal
furnished for the delectation of idlers all over the

land — and can any man say what there is more?
And the men who take part in this drama of fuss
and fustian are held up as shining lights."

"Assuredly," said the politician, "there are some
capable statesmen among all our men in high position."

"Oh, yes, they have abundance of capacity of
a certain sort. Many of them have genius for de-
bate; are brilliant leaders of faction; know admirably how to manage elections and create public
opinion—but what statesman, so called, is identified
with any principle? There is scarcely an instance
where one of them exhibits a scientific knowledge
of the subjects which he discusses; rarely an occasion where one throws light upon any of the
vexed social problems into which they thrust their
crude legislation. Who is an acknowledged authority in political economy? Who has mastered
the wages question? Who understands the operations of finance and the laws of money? Who
even understands the principles of free government?
What politician, for instance, could have written
Mill's essay on 'Liberty'? What politician anywhere analyzes, sifts, reaches the inner meaning?
Who does or can expound or explain primary principles in politics? Your politicians are almost exclusively men who desire power; who are enamored

of the public admiration that follows their useless
vocation; and they exhibit an unusual deal of skill
in obtaining and holding power. I declare emphatically that this class *must* be subordinated, must
hold a lower place in public estimation, if the people are to advance to a higher plane of intellectual
life. Men of ideas, of investigation, of scientific
training and thought, of philosophical analysis, should
fill a larger place in public thought. The politicians must be accepted as the necessary instruments
of administering government, but whose doings are
worth little more the attention now bestowed upon
them than are the enactments in a police court."

"In the administration of law, at least, we require men of the highest character; and their duties
are inferior to none."

"If our judges may be called politicians, then in
this direction politicians should suffer no abridgment
of power nor decay of influence; but the judiciary
is more scientific than political in its training; at
least it commonly has and should have the exact
scientific mind and the philosophical insight — and
with these qualities it may be safely intrusted with
the highest public duty, the administration of justice. If you argue that the makers of laws should
have no secondary rank to those who administer
laws, I reply that statute laws are commonly little

more than the cumbersome experiments of politicians, while the common law is the embodiment of
judicial analysis, and is one of the few things from
the past of endurable value.   When the limited uses
of government are recognized, the influence and
the power of the politician subordinated, and the
public intelligence directed to the study of principles rather than to the partisanship of factions,
we shall have, in my opinion, a more healthy public
sentiment and a wiser national record."

  " I see no chances of any such change," said
the politician.

  " Yes; it is likely that my hopes are father to
my thoughts.   But is it not amazing that people
are so beset with the idea that it is the province
of government to regulate everything and attempt
everything ?   Even people who admit in some degree the limitation of government, are often bent
upon government carrying out their own special
notions.   No one seems to see that, if the State
attempts any one thing beyond its legitimate duties,
it must and will attempt other things, until at last
its busy intermeddling makes a host of mischiefs.
If government, in obedience to a clamor from one
quarter, is to establish scientific schools, then it
will be urged by another class to found art-schools,
and by still another class to organize music-schools.

In undertaking the education of the people at all, there is sure to be a continual pressure upon it to carry out this or the other favorite project by people who think that government ought to be not only paternal, but paternal in the particular direction which they advocate. Some people want colleges and schools supplied by government; others want art-galleries and museums fostered by the State; others think that the theatre and the opera should have the aid of the State; still others ask why literature is not patronized by Congress; more practical people insist that canals must be dug, and railways and ships built, by government; there are still others who think that the telegraph and the express business should fall under State control; and so on, until, if all suggestions were carried out, pretty nearly the whole functions of society would be in the hands of our rulers. How is it, of all peoples, that Americans so disregard their own traditions and their own example in this matter? Have we not triumphantly shown what voluntary energies can do? Nowhere in the world is the Church so well supported, so active in its mission, so energetic and prosperous, as it is by the voluntary system in America. The Sunday-school is another example of what an immense work may be done by voluntary energies. We may be certain that the success of the voluntary method in the Church and Sunday-school gives assurance that it would also be successful for education, æsthetic culture, and all practical enterprises. The wonderful growth of America has been largely due to the fact that here more than elsewhere government gives every man free play and elbow-room. That is the whole secret of a wise government and a prosperous people. Let energies of all kinds have opportunity; regulate only those things that obstruct energy, and our future well-being is assured."

"I can at least agree with you," said the politician, "so far as regards many unwise and some dishonest projects. So long as government enters only into rightly considered schemes, into measures calculated for the good of the whole public, I can see no danger in its exercise of power. The threatening feature of our politics is the corruption that prevails in political life."

"This corruption is the inevitable consequence in republics of extended powers. Every man owns the government, he thinks, and schemes to milk it, and these schemes need not be dishonest in order to be dangerous. There is more to fear from the abundance of what may be called entirely honest schemes, than the few dishonest projects that get before our Legislatures. Dishonesty has, at its worst, strict limits. The public danger is far more urgent in those things that have the public sanction, that in themselves are commendable, that appear desirable for the public good, that enlist the enthusiasm and national pride of the people, that have the support of worthy and cultured people, that seem, on their face, eminently proper things to do. It is the multiplication of functions in desirable things that threatens the permanent security of our political institutions. I repeat with emphasis that, if there is one thing more than another our public should learn, it is the necessity of subordinating government, of withdrawing from it every function not absolutely necessary, of remanding to the domain of private enterprise the innumerable schemes continually brought before it, all calculated, however much they may be projected in the name of public good, to overweigh us with taxes, to foster lobbyism— one of the curses of the country—to increase bribery and corruption, to render legislation a means of serving innumerable personal ends, and by these hurtful influences, as well as by many practical injurious effects, to retard our prosperity, if not to destroy our institutions. Let us have done with it all. Can you not agree with me ? "

"Where, then, sir, would be my vocation ? "

"Where, indeed ? "

XI

MR. BLUFF AS AN ARITHMETICIAN.

(In the Laboratory.)

MR. BLUFF AND A BELIEVER IN INFINITESIMAL DOSES.

Bluff. So you still adhere to the Hahnemann theory of infinitesimal doses. Is it as popular as ever?

Believer. More and more popular. It grows in favor every day, but perhaps there is not such general adherence to high dilutions.

Bluff. What are high dilutions?

Believer. From the hundredth to the two hundredth. The larger number of practitioners, however, probably do not go beyond the thirtieth decimal trituration.

Bluff. Decimal triturations! It was once altogether centesimal triturations, was it not?

Believer. There is possibly a little modification here. The decimal is superseding the centesimal.

Bluff. But that is a big change, between tens

and hundreds. However, if one believes in these triturations, he is not likely to care much whether his drug comes through a hogshead or so of water more or less.

Believer. Hogsheads of water? Why do you exaggerate in this unfair manner?

Bluff. Exaggerate? Let us look into your charge a little. Drugs, you say, are attenuated through thirty dilutions—we will not explore the region of the high potencies. Now, what is a dilution? To begin, what is the first decimal dilution?

Believer. One grain of a drug, or the mother-tincture, diluted in nine drops of alcohol or water.

Bluff. So I understand. And the second dilution is a drop of the first dilution in nine drops of alcohol or water—let us say water. And the third is a drop of the second similarly diluted through nine parts of water; and the fourth is a drop of the third similarly attenuated, and so on. Am I right?

Believer. Distinctly so.

Bluff. I am delighted to hear you say so. Are you in a humor for a little arithmetic? Out with your pencil, then, and set down how many drops of water are required for the thirtieth dilution—that is, how many drops of water would be required if we carried *the whole of the mother-tincture* through thirty attenuations. It is ten drops for the first—that is, the tincture and the water make ten—a hundred in the second, a thousand in the third.

Believer. Quite right.

Bluff. Yes ; it is exactly so. We continue to multiply by ten. The fourth dilution makes 10,000 drops; the fifth 100,000. But we may as well jump the intermediate dilutions and set down 1,000,000,-000,000,000,000,000,000,000,000 drops as the requisite number for the thirtieth—being just one nonillion, that being the term for the eleventh group of numeral orders. I am afraid a good many hogsheads of water would be required to hold this number of drops. Have you a liquid scale at hand?

Believer. Not at the moment.

Bluff. That is unfortunate, for you will have to take my word for it that there are 61,440 drops in a gallon. Now, the large Croton Reservoir—

Believer. The Croton Reservoir! What are you driving at?

Bluff. Wait and see. The capacity of the great Croton Reservoir in Central Park is one billion and thirty million gallons : 1,030,000,000 multiplied by 61,440 give us, as a result, 63,283,200,000,000, or, let us say in round numbers, sixty-three trillions of drops of water. This is the contents in drops of the reservoir. It is a large number, but a glance at the two lines of figures shows us at once that it is not nearly enough for the thirty dilutions. How many reservoirs will give it, then? Let us divide our one nonillion by these sixty-three trillions, and see. Can you carry the figures in your mind's eye? Let me set them down for you. Here they are: 1,000,000,000,000,000,000,000,000,000,000, divided by 63,000,000,000,000, give us— Wonder of wonders!

Believer. Well, what is it? Give us the figures, and not exclamations.

Bluff. For my part, they take my breath away. For, my dear sir, in order to put a drop of mother-tincture—the whole drop, understand—through thirty dilutions, we should need nearly *sixteen quadrillion* RESERVOIRS of the capacity of that in Central Park! Here are the exact figures—15,873,015,873,015,873, and a fraction. This is dilution with a vengeance.

Believer. Can there be so much fresh water on the continent?

Bluff. *So much fresh water on the continent!* My good sir, you have little idea of what this amount of water means. In fact, it is impossible for the human mind to grasp a number so large as this; so let us see if we can express the amount of liquid required in larger bulks with fewer numerals. I do not know the area of the Central Park reservoir, but upon the map it appears to be about half a mile in extent in one direction, and a little less in the other, but it tapers somewhat toward one end. Now, if we estimate that a mile square would contain five such reservoirs, we are pretty close to the facts—sufficiently so for our present purpose. The geographers estimate the entire surface of the world to be about two hundred million square miles. The surface of the world is, then, capable of containing one billion reservoirs like that of Central Park. But we want space for over fifteen billion such reservoirs; and to hold this number you will find that we should absolutely require 15,873,015 worlds, and a fraction ! Here are the figures. Nearly sixteen million worlds, the entire surface of each being covered with water.

Believer. But the Croton Reservoir is comparatively shallow.

Bluff. Not more than fifty or sixty feet deep—let us say fifty feet. Let us therefore deepen our billion reservoirs standing on the surface of the globe, until they extend downward to the center, becoming, say, four thousand miles deep, that being about one half the diameter of the earth at the equator. This will increase their capacity some four hundred and twenty-two thousand times (that is, would do so if their area were uniformly maintained); so that, if the world were composed wholly of water, it would require, at the very least, roughly calculated, *more than forty worlds* in order to obtain one nonillion drops of water—that is, understand, to put the mother-tincture through thirty decimal dilutions. If the world were a cube instead of a sphere, a tolerably exact calculation could be given : it would then require nearly thirty-eight worlds of water; as it is, if we say forty-five, we shall understate the number, but a few worlds of water more or less are of no moment. Now, remember that for every dilution we must multiply the preceding sum by ten. It would thus require four hundred and fifty worlds of water for the thirty-first dilution; four thousand five hundred for the thirty-second, and so on, the fortieth dilution needing four hundred and fifty billion worlds of water!! If the twenty million stars which the great telescopes reveal in the heavens were all composed of liquid, they would not nearly supply water enough, unless averaging twenty-two thousand five hundred times larger than our world, to put one drop of tincture through forty dilutions—and yet people are constantly cured by doses of the one-hundredth dilution !

Believer. This is preposterous !

Bluff. So it is—but the figures are approximately correct, nevertheless. Verify them for yourself. But understand, it is easy enough to get the thirtieth dilution. Thirty vials, containing ten drops of water each, would enable you to do so—but a drop from the thirtieth vial would be equivalent to one nonillionth of the original drug.

Believer. You are in some way altogether out, for homœopathy is brilliantly successful.

Bluff. My dear sir, the vital principle of homœopathy is *similia similibus curantur*—"like cures like" —as we all know, and practitioners may at their pleasure give doses from the crude drug to the two hundredth dilution. I therefore say nothing about homœopathy — indeed, I find no fault with infinitesimal doses, if anybody likes them. I should prefer myself ten drops of the thirtieth dilution to ten drops too much of any drug you may name. I affirm nothing; I deny nothing — I have simply amused myself with a few figures, that is all.

XII

MR. BLUFF'S MEDITATIONS IN AN ART-GALLERY.

BACHELOR BLUFF, *solus.*

—— " I THINK I am a lover of art, but how tiresome is the ceaseless cant about its divine and elevating character! Has any of the arts—sculpture, painting, architecture, even music or poetry — ever exercised an elevating influence upon a people? Absolutely, we have only to look back to see that purely art-loving peoples have been among the most cruel, vicious, and morally degraded of all civilized communities. If one looks at Italy, where art in its varied forms has been more dominant and pervading than in any other country in the world, he can not fail to suspect that art, instead of elevating a people, may lend itself with fatal facility to their decline. The real basis of every people's advance, after all, is the diffusion of knowledge. Art with a people of intellectual activity and culture falls into its due and proper place, which is that of a graceful fringe to civilization. It indisputably supplies ideas and pleasurable sensations, and gives to character some of its most agreeable qualities; without it, life would be barren and harsh enough. But the suitable comprehension and appropriation of art come only with intellectual culture. With people who are slothful and ignorant, it relaxes fiber, fills the imagination with dreams and sensuous pictures, and helps to render the whole nature a chaos of emotions and passions. However admirable sensibility in an individual may seem, nothing is more true that in eras or with peoples where the untrained imagination has sway, human nature exhibits strange phases of depravity. Religion itself succumbs to it, and moral principles are converted into æsthetic ecstasies. There is only one real basis of advancement, and that is intellectual—the increase of knowledge, the domination of reason over imagination, the subordination of feeling and emotion to the judgment.

—— "Then, there is the spiritual element in art, of which some critics write. Is there such a thing? Is spiritualism in art anything more than a vague sentiment, a piece of transcendental ecstasy? Art, no doubt, is capable of exercising no little power over our emotional susceptibilities, but it is no new thing to imagine that our sensuous emotions have their birth in the spirit, and are a form of divine exaltation. Beauty and harmony move us greatly; there is, indeed, something strange and subtile in the delightful sensations which measured sound and harmonies of color and line awaken in us, but it is quite possible that, if the spirit of man were wholly freed from the influences and seductions of the senses, color and sound would cease to agitate it, or physical beauty have any meaning for it. One does not find the races with whom or the epochs in which spiritual life has been the most exalted falling under the dominion of art; nor have persons of the finest spiritual strain shown either the need or much of the influence of art. Art charms only the human side of us. Perhaps the Quakers, in their rigid exclusion of music and color from their spiritual exercises, are philosophically right. But they shut music and color out from their lives altogether. Possibly men and women who live in a perpetual inward light can do this, but mortals generally live through the senses. Symonds speaks of art becoming from the time of Giotto to Raphael the sole exponent of the overmastering religious emotions of the age; but was it not far more truly an exponent of the passion for a sensuous form of religion rather than for its spiritual bliss—for the pomp, the music, the color, the splendor of a grand pictorial worship, rather than for inner light and grace? The Renaissance was a grand revival of art, but the Reformation was a grander spiritual awakening, in the heat of which art and all the emotions that art excites were consumed. I can not sympathize with that form of religious fervor that fortifies the sensibilities against beauty; but there is no denying the fact that intense spiritual life renders everything else in the world valueless. It rises to a plane to which art with all its manifold seductions can not rise. And this is also true of pure intellectual life. Sound and color have very little fascination, I fancy, for the mind engrossed in the study of great problems, or deeply concerned in any pursuit of an engrossing character. Neither great reformers nor great thinkers have exhibited much susceptibility to art, at least in its forms of painting and sculpture.

"But art nevertheless has great control over the human heart. Has it more than beauty in nature has? Are the emotions that it awakens in any way different? When one looks upon the ravishing beauty of a 'maiden in her flower,' can it be pretended that the sensations thus awakened are—difficult as they are to analyze or to comprehend—in

any wise more than a delight of the senses—an in-
explicable emotion which color and contour, freshness and grace, have the power to excite? Does
loveliness in marble awaken emotions other than
those that loveliness in flesh stimulates, unless it be
the single one of admiration for the skill of the
copyist? It is a great temptation, no doubt, to re-
mand the strange agitations of the senses to the
spirit; they are certainly subtile and profound enough
to escape dissection; but we exalt ourselves by illu-
sions if we fall into the habit of thinking that the
delights of the senses, so often enjoyed at the cost
of spiritual purity, are really identical with the felicities of the soul. But, dear me, see how I moral-
ize, and I came simply to look at some pictures!

—— "Well, there are many pleasing pictures here,
but I have discovered in my travels more charming
natural ones. That is human nature. We are all of
us continually finding wonderful picturesque groups
and lovely compositions of colors, and begging the
artists to come and paint them for us. But the artists themselves are quite sure they have discovered
charming scenes, and wonder how the world can be
so cold and insensible. But who can see what the
artist sees—who could see what I saw in the pictures I have discovered, let them be ever so well

painted? To the artist all the pigments on his canvas are united with the life, the color, the motion of
the original scene. When he looks upon the canvas the mind acts as well as the eyes see; he perceives not so much what *is* as what he *remembers ;*
the cheeks of his painted people suffuse with color;
their eyes sparkle; the light laugh breaks from their
lips; the shadows of the trees dance and play; the
winds lift the stray locks of hair and bring delicious odors; the air is soft and sweet, and sends
tingling pleasure through the veins; of all these
things, the pigments speak to him, but they have no
such message to others, unless, indeed, a rare spirit
comes, one unusually imaginative and receptive, who
has taught himself to look behind the composition
on the canvas to the thought in the artist's mind.
This is a great limitation to art. And how complete
the limit is in portrait-painting!—for who can get a
true idea of a face from the most skillfully painted
copy of it? The likeness of a person I have known
recalls to my imagination the expression of his features, the light of his eye, his tone, and voice, and
manner; it is the operation of my own mind work-
ing in coöperation with what the painter has done
that creates the likeness—that transfuses with real
life the dead image before me. But portraits of
people we have not met are but faint images of their

originals, or they are misleading ones, as we discover if at a later time we meet them. We thus
not only see differently because of different tempera-
ments, but differently because of the absence or
presence of associated ideas. Half of the power in
a picture that moves me comes in this way from
myself.

—— "This notion is applicable to what has recently been said about the human element in landscape-painting. It is necessary, say one class of
critics, that landscape-painting should possess human interest—some connection with man's doings—
in order to give it any real or permanent hold upon
our sympathies. But does a painting really possess
human sentiment simply by putting human figures
in it? Do I care for yonder seashore because there
are figures of women and children upon the beach,
more than for this ·mountain-stream, where there
are no signs of human life? I might, perhaps, if
the figures were really human—if they touched me
in some definite way. But even critics who require
human sentiment admit that it may be accomplished
by suggestion. One of them, I remember, cites
Stanfield's ' The Abandoned '—a dismantled ship
rocking on a stormy sea—and thinks that the connection of the ship with man, the sort of semi-

humanity which the title suggests, gives a real force and interest to the painting, which waves and sky could not produce. Yes; there must be in this way, or in some way, human interest—but perhaps the most powerful human sympathy may come from associated ideas, from the memories that a painting awakens, from its power to touch the imagination or the sympathies. If a painting, for instance, of a forest interior, the solitudes of which are disturbed by no human presence, is full of imaginative power and strong sympathies—if the painter felt and expressed the scene in all its beauties and charms— the spectator identifies with it the full beat of human interest. The cool shadows are to him a dream of delicious rest; the fall of the brook over the stones sends musical murmurs to his ear; he feels the pleasant wind fan his cheek; the sunshine that flecks through the leaves charms his eye with its shifting play of light; odors from the mosses and aromatic plants seem to fill his nostrils; the scene in its completeness takes possession of his whole nature, fills him with a subdued rapture, becomes an embodiment of his emotions. If a forest-scene has no power of this kind over one's imagination, it is really less than nothing, for the value and charm of any picture must lie in its control over human thought, in its power to transport the spectator to the scene and permit him to fill it with his own personality. In this way a human element clearly often does enter landscape art effectively, efficiently, and to the complete identification of the scene with our emotions and our susceptibilities. The mere introduction of figures obviously can not of itself create human interest; if they form a part of the picture in such a way as to strengthen the sentiment of the landscape, well and good; if not, they weaken if they do not destroy the very human interest to the end of which they are imported into the scene. In fact, the value and character of a painting do not depend upon fixed rules at all, but upon the imagination of the painter, lacking which his human figures will have no human vitality or hold ; possessing which, his solemn, empty forest-depths will be full of human feeling.

—— " And yet, one longs sometimes for passionate stir in pictures. The landscapes that I have seen have great charm, but what landscape can send a passionate throb from the heart ? Viewed that way, how wearisome almost all art is ! There is an abundance of artistic device, of munificent color, of excellent execution, of agreeable ideas; but when does anything take an immense hold upon one's sympathies ? Our artists ignore the

9

aspirations, the emotions, and the passions of the
race; and yet the hold an art has upon a people
must depend upon the measure of human passion
there is in it. People haunt the galleries in search
of the greatly beautiful; they yearn for stories upon
canvas that shall fill them with exalted pleasure;
they long for the profounder passion, for the thrill
of intense sympathy. The universal hold that art
in old times held upon the people was due to intense mutual sympathies; art expressed the fervor,
the religious ecstasy, the deep-seated feelings of
the whole body of the people—now it addresses a
few *blasé* critics and jaded connoisseurs. What if
some painter should arise who painted for us great
themes in a great manner? There would be a different public in our galleries then — the passionate,
warm-hearted, large-souled multitude would be there;
such a painter would convey to the hearts of millions lessons of heroism, of fortitude, of faith, of
affection, of divine beauty. Perhaps all this is too
much for human genius. George Eliot, I recollect,
declares that 'the instances are scattered but thinly
over the galleries of Europe, in which the fortune
or selection even of the chief masters has given to
art a face at once young, grand, and beautiful.' It
is strange that youth and noble beauty should be
so difficult. Nor can I say that I much like the

grand themes of the old painters as they present them. Is it possible to be satisfied with any of the crucifixions? Some beautiful figures, some noble faces—but what forced composition in almost every instance! And as for the contorted and distorted Christs scattered throughout the Continent, they are simply appalling. The examples of physical agony found in all the old churches show the rude, bloody, melodramatic kind of art that was employed to reach and excite the people. Am I to argue, then, that the attempt now to paint great themes would end in coarse sensation? It would in some hands, no doubt; in fact, I fear the result of grand themes now as much as I hoped for them a moment ago. I remember that a 'Laughing Boy,' by Murillo, in Warwick Castle, fascinated me much more than that painter's 'Assumption' at the Louvre. But this is because the 'Assumption' is too great a theme for any human skill; and so is the 'Crucifixion'; so is the figure of Christ—but there are some grand heads of Christ, witness Correggio's and Guido's. It is impossible not to wish for a stirring, heroic art, but one feels the danger of it.

—— "Old art did certainly have some relation to currents of thought and national tendency. Now art is really as far from the people as if it were so many hieroglyphs. An English reviewer has lately written of the reflection of national character in national art. Neither in England nor here is there any such thing. There is no common ground of feeling, no common standard of judgment, no accepted basis of appreciation or interchange of ideas. The art world is a world of its own, wherein the culture, the ideas, the aspirations, are essentially different from the ideas and purposes of the rest of the community. Even literary circles have for the most part little in common with art circles, poets and writers being generally a little more ignorant of art beyond its historical phase, and more indifferent to it, than any other class. Artists here, for the most part, simply address one another, and a small circle of admirers. American painters are commonly cautious, conventional, simple-minded, with no theatrical fondness for sensation or extravagance, loving their art in its minor chords, so to speak; appreciating delicacy and purity of expression much more than stirring action. Our people, on the other hand, are bold and restless, full of invention, delighting in novelty, ambitious for great successes, audacious in conception, and inclined to emphasis and exaggeration in all that they utter. Judging from our national characteristics, we should show in our art vigorous movement, great audacity, boldness, and a passion for large themes; but how completely the reverse are the facts! The same strange contradiction is apparent in England. There is a domestic art there that is very popular, and it hits the taste of a large public, but this is only one side of the British mind. Britons scarcely less than ourselves are restless and ambitious; they push colonizing schemes into remote quarters; their ships penetrate every sea; they have shown, and are showing, immense audacity, enterprise, and a spirit of aggrandizement — all of which has some place in their writings, but scarcely any in their art. Recently English artists have exhibited a great fondness for classical subjects, the exhibitions being full of paintings of Greek and Roman scenes, and yet it would be difficult to imagine anything more radically opposed than is the rugged, picturesque, and barbaric English character to the refined Greek. French art is doubtless nearer to national character than either British or American art; but painters like Corot and Millet have nothing in common with the attributes usually accredited to French character — with those painters extravagance and theatrical sensation being utterly unknown. The fact is, the larger number of artists and writers are too often Bohemians, with erratic tastes and wholly independent modes of thought, and for these reasons, if for no other, are not always calculated by their natural bent to show the age and body of the time, its 'form and press-ure.' It is clear that national character must not be sought for in art — which is proof that art is essentially an exotic; that it lies upon the surface for the amusement of a few. To the community generally it is an idle and practically worthless thing, which may in some degree be accepted, but which has very little place in the earnest interests of life. Can there be a great national art until all this is changed ?

—— "How many vagaries art has fallen into of late! The vague, the unknown, the untranslatable, are now hotly advocated as rightful substitutes for clearness, precision, and revelation. There are critics who appear to gauge their estimate of a picture by the sum of eccentricity it displays; and we actually find undecipherable smudges held up as suitable examples of landscape-painting! It is very puzzling, and the puzzle is not less by calling these performances "impression" pictures. They certainly impress the uninstructed beholder, but not in a way to give comfort to the artist. Why, in fact, are they specially "impression" pictures ? They give impressions of nothing but of the incomprehensible; or, if they are records of impressions, a key is needed to translate them. An impression, according to some authorities, is an attempt to fix upon canvas the instantaneous impression of a scene—to catch a changing mood of feeling, a fleeting touch of color, a vanishing light, a sudden insight or grasp —in other words, to take a landscape on the wing, as it were. If it were possible to do this well, perhaps something would be accomplished worth the effort. But wherein do transitory impressions differ from permanent ones? In the complex action of the mind, it is impossible, even in an instantaneous impression of an object, to obliterate the host of associations and the sum of experiences gathered there. We know the human features so well that the most rapid glance at a face conceivable is sure to bring before us all the parts—the eyes, the cheeks, the nose, the mouth, all are sure to distinctly appear, if not in actual vision at least by associations that are inseparable from the vision. The flash of lightning that reveals a figure reveals it to our mental impressions complete. Each of us knows a tree so well, carries in his mind its color, its construction, its play of light and shade, that the eye, sweeping over a forest in the swiftest manner possible, will inevitably have just as instantaneously an impression of the forms of the trees, their spread of bough, their recesses of shadow, their leaves gleaming and quivering in the light, as it has of the fact that there are trees there at all. To think of a tree is to think of something defined, of something possessing known characteristics ; and under no circumstances, I am convinced, would it be possible for the human vision to catch a glimpse of trees so swiftly as to make them seem anything less, or anything different, or anything more, than just what they are. It will be said that we do not, in fact, see the complete tree under such circumstances, but only think we do. This makes no difference, for it is with what *seems* that art has solely to do. It is not dealing with the science of optics, but with appearances.

—— " The impressionists, it seems, condemn *finish* in pictures. No doubt an ignorant notion prevails that smoothness and polish are the crowning qualities of a picture, and this form of emasculated prettiness should be denounced. But people who rush to the extreme of preferring rudeness and slap-dash to that true finish which completes and helps to render perfect, commit as absurd an error of judgment. There is a kind of finish which every one is entitled to expect in a work of art—the sort of finish found in the great masters. Artists of all schools and critics of all varieties of caprice have no difficulty in admiring Rubens, Raphael, Murillo, Titian, Vandyck, and the host of great painters. There is no dispute in regard to these painters as to what is 'finish' and what is not; their paintings are felt to be complete; they are vital, they are rich in texture and color, definite as to form, satisfying as to drawing; they take possession of us fully; they give no opportunity for men to say they are lacking, whether in force or in finish. What new dogma is this, then, that, so long as color is heaped on in a vigorous manner, a picture must be accepted as complete, however crude and raw it may seem, however absolute is the evidence that the artist stopped before he had done?

"And their lack of finish is nine times out of ten simply inability to *give* finish. The sketches of almost every artist show indications of skill; the beginnings of art are always easy. It is only when sketches are developed into pictures that the full resources of the artist, his limitations as well as his resources, are made known. Many a sketch indicates breadth, freedom, ease, virility : the difficulty is, how to carry these qualities on to their legitimate end ; how to do more than indicate and suggest— that is, how to *perform*. In every art just this difficulty arises. Many are the poets that have good ideas, readiness, abundant invention ; but very few

are the poets who attain sufficient mastery over their
art to give the last finish, the touch of completeness,
to their work; and it is just this touch of completeness, this supreme finish, that separates great poetry
from inferior poetry.   The lesser poets are not so
deficient in ideas as they are in knowledge of their
art—that is, how to complete.   There are thousands
of stories and romances written that show lively imagination, considerable invention, good native talent
—but how few that come up to the high standard
of finish and completeness that alone make greatness!   Any sculptor can model the outlines of a
figure; apprentices do this much in every Italian
atelier ; it is exactly in and by *finish* that the accomplished master steps in and lifts the work to perfection.   Painting is not different from the other arts
in this particular.   Every recognized great painting
that exists is 'finished'; every painting, in order to
be great or worthy, *must* be finished — not made
smooth or polished, of course, but brought to that
state of completeness that the methods and processes
of the work are hidden, so that one who looks at it
sees textures and not paint, force by nature of completeness and not by ruggedness, things and not
guesses at things.

——— " But, after all, why should there be theories

—why fixed, preconceived notions? If a man has anything to declare in art or letters, let him choose his own methods. Criticism here is apt to be simply impertinent. It is one's duty to stand before any work of art solely to receive impressions—not to formulate laws, but to discover intentions. I surrender myself, therefore, to these paintings; I banish from my mind all prejudices, all preconceived notions, all forms of self-assertion. Let them impress me, each in its own way and to its own end. Let them awaken in me the sense of beauty, stir my fancy, fill me with some emotion, reveal some truth, produce what impression they can. Willing as I am, they should certainly justify their being in some way. Is it I that am cold and insensible, or the paintings that are meaningless? There must be something more than willingness, doubtless, to understand a painting; knowledge, perhaps, is necessary in order that one may understand what the painter means, and thus derive right impressions. Knowledge, indisputably, is necessary in order to comprehend how effects are produced, but why should it be necessary simply to feel effects? How much knowledge is necessary to appreciate the splendor of a sunset? How much to feel the beauty of the sky, or of a rose? Very likely cultivation has done something for us in developing susceptibility to the beauties of Nature, but there is no class excluded from her. Every person with a little native imagination delights in the colors and forms that she produces on her grand canvases. If it needs no inculcation in subtile mysteries to see the beauties of Nature, why does it in art? If I have susceptibility in the galleries of the forests, and thus fall under the influence of glancing lights and mellowed vistas, assuredly the beauties that the painters reproduce ought to influence me also. It requires knowledge to read accurately and freely *all* that a painter puts in his painting, but, if he has unmistakably expressed true beauty there, very few are incapable of seeing it and feeling it in some degree. There must be response in him that looks, but there must be force in him that produces. If after I have surrendered myself fully to a painting, and it fails to awaken sensations, then I may inquire why—and here criticism legitimately steps in. If the artist has ideas, let us accept them, whether we quite agree with them or not, and be silent; if he has not ideas, then we are masters, not he, and may demand an account."

XIII

MR. BLUFF ON MELANCHOLY.

(On a Yacht, on a Moonlit Evening.)

MIRANDA,
BACHELOR BLUFF,
OSCAR.

"I LOVE moonlight," said Miranda, "and especially moonlight on the water—it is so melancholy
and sweet."

"And you like, no doubt," said Mr. Bluff, a little
sarcastically, "melancholy music, to make all in
keeping. I dare say you are fond of imagining
yourself Jessica, sitting with Lorenzo and listening to his soft murmur about the moonlight sleeping
upon the bank, and the sounds of music, and touches of sweet harmony, etc. You could, I am sure,
repeat the whole passage now, if put to it."

"What sentimental young lady could not?" remarked Oscar, as he touched lightly with his finger
the ashes on his cigar.

"Or sentimental young gentleman," retorted Miranda. "Were there ever lovers that did not read that passage together? I believe I can count a dozen melancholy young gentlemen who, in moonlight walks or sails, have whispered in my ear, 'How sweet the moonlight sleeps upon this bank!'"

"It is a very pretty piece of poetry," said Mr. Bluff, "and Shakespeare then was in his best poetical mood. But I am not fond of moonlight, or of melancholy in any of its forms Give me the splendor of the sun, and Nature when she is joyous."

"I thought," replied Miranda, "that all old bachelors are melancholy. I should say it would be natural to them."

"It is very perverse and wrong-headed in me, no doubt, not to be sad and melancholy," said Mr. Bluff. "It is rather a reflection on your sex, I confess, who are disposed to believe that all old bachelors must inevitably be unhappy. I think myself that it is very ungrateful for us to persist in being happy when so many lovely women are anxious to be the source of our bliss."

"If lovely women," remarked Oscar, who was gazing abstractedly at the moon, "have the power to expel melancholy, their services are likely in the future to be greatly esteemed. The world, you know, is declared to be growing melancholy. Over-civilization is making the educated classes everywhere

despondent and sad. Why should it do so, I wonder?"

"Is it true," asked Mr. Bluff, "that over-civilization is the cause? Would wise and worthy civilization—civilization of the right kind and character
—increase the melancholy of the world?"

"One can not easily say what different conditions would bring about," replied Oscar, "but civilization such as exists seems to be producing great
weariness of life. It is a disease eating into the
heart of society. It is intense in Russia, where a
dreamy melancholy is described by native writers as
one of the features of cultured circles; and a similar
melancholy is said to be spreading over England.
Some of the magazines are making it a theme for
discussion, and the poets have fallen into the vein."

"Poets and romancists," said Mr. Bluff, "have
always been rather disposed to take despairing views
of things; and melancholy, you know, has been
sometimes cultivated as a fashion. Young Arthur
in ' King John ' exclaims:

> "'. . . when I was in France,
> Young gentlemen would be as sad as night,
> Only for wantonness.'

This sort of affectation, however, is as old as human nature. Then there is the whimsical egotism

and selfish bitterness of the Jaques type, a melancholy not unlike that the poets affect, and which has been well characterized as 'Werthcrism.' Then there is the moonlight melancholy which young ladies affect."

"We do not affect," exclaimed Miranda, with spirit, "we really feel it. I believe that all people with poetry and tenderness in their nature are subject to melancholy moods; of course, tough old bachelors are notoriously without either of those qualities."

"Then, young lady, we are just the physicians to prescribe for the complaint."

"It is not a complaint—it is a poetic ecstasy."

"Melancholy ecstasies of the young-lady kind are not going to do much harm. But there is a spirit of melancholy abroad, as Oscar says, which needs sharp treatment in order to effect a cure. There are many persons who suffer from a constitutional tendency to melancholy, but the people who write about it, who burst into pathetic rhymes, who go about mooning over the sadness and misery of life, are a set of idle and egotistic dreamers who either cultivate melancholy as a supposed sign of poetic genius, or who are oppressed with *ennui* from pure idleness, or whose melancholy is simply a reaction from dissipation. All such fellows should be

well whipped to some honest, wholesome task. A
few earnest things to do, a little subordination of
their diseased self-love, some small control over their
appetites, would send their affectations and their
whims to the winds."

"Still, sir," replied Oscar, "I must think there is
a great deal of genuine sadness in the world."

"You are right," replied Mr. Bluff. "But is
this sadness increased by culture and intellectual
development? Has the world grown graver because
it has grown wiser?"

"There is more meditation and study, a higher
ideal of life, a greater mental strain, and these
things have combined to produce a peculiar schol-
arly melancholy. Years ago Emerson found in England numbers of what he called 'silent Greeks,'
men whose fastidious culture shrank from the collisions and contests of life, whose over-fastidious-
ness had paralyzed impulse and ambition, who admired nothing and sought for nothing, because
nothing could come up to the level of their high
ideals."

"Still, is it true that sadness is specially the
product of culture?" asked Mr. Bluff. "You have
seen, of course, Millet's pictures of French rustics.
They are the very incarnation of melancholy. What
a picture of sullen gloom is that of his 'Sower'—a

life without hope, without light, bound for ever to
the wheel of dreary task! And yet this is an out-
of-door laborer. We might expect melancholy to
grow up in the shop amid the ceaseless din of
machinery, but in primitive, picturesque labor why
should there not abound the old joyousness? There
is less oppression and injustice now: the laborer is
protected; the fruits of his fields are garnered for
himself, instead of for priest, king, or robber baron;
and yet, if we may believe the painter, an intense
gloom rests upon him. Can it be that, suffering
less than his ancestors, he yet embodies the accu-
mulations of sorrow and despair that have been
borne by his race? Or is it that, while still as
lowly as his progenitors, he has caught visions of
higher and better things, that time has taught him
to think and compare, to discover all that is with-
held from him, to see in himself the perpetual drudge
kept for ever in the dust by the unjust discrimina-
tions of life? The English rustic, also, has ceased
to be the merry fellow he was once — foregone all
his old sports and pastimes, without really gaining
compensation in education; but, having in a rude
way learned to think, he has come into the possession of discontent and distrust. It is no wonder
that gloom should be the heritage of drudges of
the fields and victims of tasteless labor; but a won-

der, indeed, that education should bring a mildew upon the heart and brain of people who have all the world before them to choose from and enjoy. Can you explain this? "

" I confess that I can not."

" If it is true," continued Mr. Bluff, "it is because education is wrong in its methods and objects. It would be different, I suspect, if Nature were studied more and the artificial sentiments of the poets and romancists less. Melancholy often comes of brooding and introspection, and hence if men were to look abroad rather than within, to open their eyes and hearts to the beauties and wonders of meadows and woods, of sky and sea, their despondency would be effectually exorcised. It is not knowledge simply, but kinds of knowledge, that bring gloom and sadness. I have not discovered that philosophers, historians, poets, naturalists, men of science, or men of intellectual out-of-door pursuits, have any special tendency to melancholy. Indeed, the great lights in all literature for the most part have been men of serene and happy natures. If Dante and Cowper and Dr. Johnson were melancholy men, Shakespeare and Goethe and Scott and a vast number of others, eminent in all branches of letters, were not. Every form of healthful mental occupation brings to the mind joy rather than gloom

or sorrow; and melancholy, excepting for the moment all who are constitutionally afflicted with it, so
far as it is the product at all of intellectualism, is
the result of unhealthful forms of it. Every strain
upon the emotions produces a morbid reaction; and
this is why certain poets and all writers who force
themselves into ecstasies of feeling suffer when the
mental intoxication is over. Severe occupations that
employ but do not excite the mind — whether low
or high in degree—leave no taint of melancholy behind. It is not those persons who think most, nor
those who are most keenly alive to the sorrows and
misfortunes that befall mankind, that are overcome
by sadness, but commonly the minds that work upon
their sensibilities and feelings, that cultivate melancholy by the emotions. No doubt all such persons
have at the beginning a tendency to melancholy,
but, instead of cultivating cheerfulness, they have
cultivated disease."

"They have simply, Mr. Bluff," interrupted Miranda, "obeyed the impulses of their hearts. I do
not wonder that poets and men of genius are melancholy, for their exquisite perceptions, their refined
culture, must make them weary of the common
things of life."

"Culture, excellent young lady, ought to chasten
and enrich our whole being, filling us with Matthew

Arnold's 'sweetness and light.' Is it not odd, now, that one prophet should be preaching this benefi- cence as the outcome of the right use of the mind, while others are deploring the gloom that intellect- ualism is casting over the world? But, in fact, is it intellectualism? Are we not giving that name to emotional unrest, self-consciousness, and feverish de- sire? True intellectualism broadens, enlarges, ex- alts; all great, honest, healthful mental training and development can do no one harm."

"But you speak," said Oscar, "of Dr. Johnson's melancholy, whose mental occupations were certainly of a robust and healthful character."

"I excepted those who are constitutionally af- flicted with melancholy."

"But are not all people suffering under habitual depression of mind simply victims to a constitu- tional disorder? In its extreme phase melancholy becomes a form of insanity, and one which physi- cians set down as among the most obstinate and difficult of cure."

"I believe," replied Mr. Bluff, "that with all truly healthful persons—healthful in mind as well as in body—joyousness is the natural, spontaneous, inevitable expression of their being. To breathe, to move, to live, are in themselves pleasure and hap- piness with all well-organized persons. There may bc trials, sorrows, sufferings, misfortuncs, even bitter experiences; but, so long as a healthful balance is maintained throughout the being, the spirit rebounds from these sufferings, and begins to weave hopeful promises for the future. No outward circumstance determines the cheerfulness or the sadness of men —the rich may be sad and the poor cheerful, the fortunate may be gloomy and the unfortunate full of hope, the sick may be full of the spirit of joy and the strong wrapped up in morbid gloom. I have heard stalwart fellows deploring in lachrymose strains the misery of life in the very presence of confirmed invalids whose cheerfulness shed radiance upon all within their circle. Some persons are victims of dyspepsia, the most joy-killing of all ailments; some are victims of diseases that cast shadows upon the soul; some are cursed with a constitutional inclination to sadness. The causes are various, but every case of melancholy is the product of some defect in the organization. Melancholy is the sign of disease, and a capacity for cheerfulness hence is nothing more than supreme good health—good health of mind even more than of body. As a disease, then, it should be treated, and every effort made to cast it out, just as is made with other forms of sickness; very much, indeed, can be done to eradicate it when there is a will to do so.

Cheerfulness ought to be placed among the cardinal virtues, and its cultivation made incumbent upon every one as a duty."

"I like cheerfulness well enough," pouted Miranda; "but, if you are going to make it a duty, then I shall *not* like it. Duties are never agreeable; it is only when things are pleasures that one cares for them."

"But why has melancholy increased?" asked Oscar. "Admitting all you say to be true, it does not explain why sadness should be affecting the race in the way it does."

"It is due to the increase of sedentary habits and the low order of physical health that has come therefrom; to indigestion and other diseases that come from neglect of exercise; and additionally to a fondness for introspective, subjective study of passions, and to the general hot-house atmosphere of our emotional literature, to which I referred before. I half suspect, however, that dyspepsia is the most active cause—or, rather, dyspepsia comes from the other causes, and melancholy from it. Nothing so clouds the mind and affects the spirits as this disorder. Only recently I heard of an instance of one who had been for many years a victim to dyspepsia, and suffered in consequence from the gloom and depression that accompanied it. But the time came when this illness passed off, and eventually he became a sufferer from gout. But great was the change. His spirits rose with the pain; his cheerfulness became proverbial."

"Must I get the gout, sir," asked Oscar, "in order to be rid of melancholy?"

"Good, sharp suffering would cure you, I am sure; or any severe duty, or high purpose, or great responsibility. Even men constitutionally disposed to melancholy are likely to be cured by some form of heroic treatment. In one way or another get a cheerful habit of mind, and one good thing to this end is a cheerful and robust literature. Matthew Arnold tells us of the extraordinary power with which Wordsworth feels the joy offered to us in nature, and the joy offered to us in the simple elementary affections and duties. Here is a supreme test of the worth of all poetry, of all literature of the imagination, and of all art. There is really no reason for the existence of anything within the scope designated that does not fill the heart with joy, that does not counteract the whole array of evils that make melancholy. I do not hesitate to make this assertion, hard and uncompromising as it may seem. Carried into effect, such an edict would sweep out of existence some very beautiful fables, no doubt, but, as our sympathy for the sad fate of the Leanders and Romeos of story is really born of our previous joy in their being, we need not deprive the world of imagination of these pathetic legends. But romance and poetry and art that do not awaken in us thrills of pleasure, that do not deepen our delight in the world and in mankind, that do not afford us sweet morsels for meditation and appropriation, should be shut out from the light altogether —thrust back into the domains of darkness and unhealthful passion whence they came. What other possible mission should poetry and the arts have than to increase the happiness of mankind? If they fail to do this, if they cause unrest rather than rest, pain rather than delight, disease rather than health, they are simply an enemy of the race. I realize very well the sweetness of a sad strain in music and the righteous sympathy that sorrow awakens; these are things that soften and subdue our grosser passions and fill up the measure of our being, but they are quite different from the gloom in which melancholy people are enshrouded, which is commonly selfish rather than sympathetic, full of bitterness rather than sweetness. But, however this may be, inasmuch as happiness is the legitimate end of existence, the sole thing that makes it desirable or endurable, the worth of everything is determinable by its contribution to this end, and by this test alone

10

should knowledge, progress, culture, literature, art, be measured."

"Well," muttered Miranda, as she wrapped herself closely in a shawl, and turned her eyes to the moon, "the sermon has been a long one. All the same, I like melancholy poetry, and melancholy music, and melancholy moonlight."

XIV

MR. BLUFF ON MORALS IN LITERATURE AND NUDITY IN ART.

(Over Wine and Walnuts.)

BACHELOR BLUFF,
MR. QUIVER.

Quiver (*poet, novelist, essayist, translator of Baudelaire, and disciple of Swinburne*). We claim for our art, sir, the privilege of covering the whole field of human thought, feeling, and experience. No literature, sir, is a great literature that does not sound the depths of woe and reach the heights of ecstasy—that does not reflect human sufferings and express human aspirations, and embody all that men and women feel and enjoy, endure and hope. The exclusion of passions because they are wrong passions, or of acts because they are criminal acts, is simply to emasculate literature.

Bluff (*energetically*). That is to say, that while in life and society, and in all forms of intercourse between men, some things are forbidden, literature is privileged to descant upon everything and uncover everything—that it has no sacred reserves, that it is bound by no discrimination between clean and unclean, that it is just as much its province to excite wrong as it is to stimulate rightful emotions.

Quiver. The only morals, sir, that art is concerned with is fidelity to one's own perceptions, and faithfulness to artistic truth. This form of morality we enforce. The worker who surrenders his convictions to popular clamor, or who descends from a pure art-ideal to an inferior standard in order to win the appreciation of the multitude, is, in our judgment, immoral. It is wholly a question of fidelity to what one feels and sees.

Bluff. It is supremely, sir, a question of good to mankind. Artists and poets must be honest, but there is nothing to prevent them from being also discreet; and it is not a law of honesty that everything must be said. Art has the whole broad field of life and nature before it, but its duty in this wide area is to *select.* The question of morals may be so far eliminated that beauty may be the exclusive aim of art; its purpose may be rightfully limited to the production of pleasurable sensations. It is true that a well-painted landscape, or a piece of elevated, harmonious verse, or a fine statue, or a noble piece of architecture, has each that subtile morality which all things possess that lift up the imagination and fill us with the sense of beauty. But all these things are without distinct ethical purpose, and art generally may be similarly freed from any primary necessity of morals—that is, it may be wholly æsthetic in its inspiration and in its aim. But it is not privileged, sir, on the other hand, to be *im*moral, directly or by implication. Its business is to select, to discover and portray the beautiful, the elevated, the ennobling, the pleasurable; to stir the emotions of pity and sympathy, to excite admiration and emulation, to enlarge the boundary of experience and sensation; but it is not its function to deal with the repulsive and horrible, to act upon morbid and unhealthful passions, to excite contempt for sacred or rightful things, to appeal to gross or sensual appetites, to deal with the foul and diseased things of life. However strenuous an upholder of the largeness and freedom of art you may be, you must see that it is under obligation to select, to exclude, to separate the fit from the unfit.

Quiver. Yes; but wholly on artistic grounds. There are limitations and reserves, but the artist, and not the moralist, knows accurately what these are. The artist excludes the gross, the barbaric, the crude, and the physically repulsive; but everything that takes place in the heart of man is his. One difficulty which we encounter in this country is the notion that literature should not treat of subjects of which the young and innocent should be kept in ignorance. This is absurd. Books are written for men and women, and not for green boys and girls. The American public in this matter is as feeble and squeamish as a prudish old maid.

Bluff. The American public, sir, is, in fact, the least squeamish public of any.

Quiver. You astonish me when you say that!

Bluff. Nevertheless it is true, and I will prove it. The example of France is constantly held up by your school, where pictorial art is pagan in its devotion to the nude, and literature wholly free in the selection of its themes and in its treatment of them. And yet the French public in one way is very squeamish: it permits its authors to touch upon every subject, but then it banishes their writings out-of-doors. The novel there, for instance, scarcely enters respectable families at all; no young girl is permitted access to it, and even elders in the more serious classes will not touch it. It is the same with the theatre, from which young women particularly are excluded on account of the themes taken up by the dramatists. In France a young woman is watched over at every step; not a book is placed in her hands that is not first examined; not a soul

is permitted to breathe a word in her ear upon
any topic without the knowledge of her guardians.
She knows neither literature, nor art, nor the world;
she is educated under the most exacting and watchful " squeamishness " possible.   With us, on the contrary, the novel, and the magazines with their many
stories, enter every house, they lie on every cen-
ter-table, they are as accessible to the girl of sixteen as to the man of sixty, and the majority of
their readers is composed of the female sex.   We
throw open our libraries to every class; we teach
our children to be readers; we cover our library-
tables in confidence with the fresh issues from the
press, and we discuss freely with our wives, sons, and
daughters, the qualities of new novels and new poems.   What has followed is just what any wise man
would have predicted; for, whenever and wherever
women become readers, license of speech and many
themes are driven out of literature.   The French
have as keen a sense of the moral and immoral as
any people in the world, but they have an extraordinary notion that ignorance and innocence go together, and that as soon as one has learned the nature of vice he may be permitted to indulge in his
salacious tastes at pleasure.   The application of this
theory to women — that matrons being no longer
ignorant have lost the instincts of innocence and

modesty—is horrible.   But to go back, sir—is not the American squeamishness which insists that literature shall be pure and accessible to young and old alike, far more rational, not to say honorable, than that French squeamishness which permits great license to its writers, and then reads their productions in secret?   This is a confession that there are subjects forbidden to art—and this is all American squeamishness affirms.

Quiver. But do not things become proper or improper according to conditions?   There are passions which the young should not surmise, but of which the mature can not be ignorant.

Bluff. Why should the mature, tell me, inflame their imaginations by pictures of these passions? Literature, sir, would be far more sweet and wholesome if the darker passions of our kind were altogether eliminated from it.   Those productions, sir, are best in every sense which lead us away from the heated atmosphere of the emotions; that either fill us with high ideas and lofty principles, or cheer us by gay and enlivening pictures of life.   And specially the whole range of passions and incidents growing out of improper or illicit love is unclean, and has no rightful place in literature.

Quiver. But these passions are the most powerful of all the passions, and they afford some of the most thrilling opportunities for an artist's purpose. The French dramatists, for instance, believe that the heart which yields to temptation and which struggles to recover its social place by reform and exemplary conduct appeals to human sympathy with an intensity unequaled by any other situation. Ordinary crimes can not supply the conditions needed for the dramatist's deep purpose. The offense must be one which society declares to be unpardonable. It must be one that has arrayed against it the traditions and instincts and prestiges of the world. There can be no great situation of this kind if the crime be of a venial character. The dramatist, therefore, seizes upon a woman who has sinned vilely, and then essays to show that profound and sustained repentance must win and does win the sympathy even of those who have proclaimed the moral degradation of the offense. It is a conflict between the stern justice of society and the merciful sympathies of the individual that gives to the condemned French dramas their great hold upon the public mind. It is this conflict, with its vivid contrasts, its effective combinations of mingled impulses and feelings, that takes such a deep hold upon the dramatic instincts of the French playwriters, and gives to their vivid invention characters and stories so eminently susceptible of intense human passion. It is a bold but not an immoral grasp of conditions veined through and through with tragic possibilities. It is the distinct assertion that an art dealing with the human heart must not be excluded from a domain that includes affection, and passion, and remorse, and struggle, and woe, and hope, in their widest reach and deepest power.

Bluff. I can conceive of such a struggle as this so presented as to meet nearly all the requirements of the purists. Much depends, however, upon the fact whether vices are treated really as vices, and sins as sins, and not so glozed over as to look half like virtues. Let the sympathies be unmistakably for the sinner and not for the sin. But while plays and books of this kind may possibly be condoned, they do not make great literature; they do not exalt, they do not refine, they do not enrich and sweeten, and make happy, the heart of the world. They are simply intellectual stimulants—and it is because they inflame and excite, because they enlist the passions and emotions in full force, that their hold upon the multitude is so great. If any possible result can come of them it must be in their influence as deterrents, and this is not an artistic but a moral function—the very thing you denounce. For my part, I am inclined not only to condemn the passionate literature of the modern French school, but much more besides, even among the world's classics. What end is served in any sense, moral or artistic, by the jealous furies of Othello or the bloody plottings of Macbeth? The mental tribulations of Hamlet enlist our sympathies and afford matter for intellectual study, but how much finer and worthier the story would be were there a little less killing! I do not object to tragic emotions when associated with high purpose or righteous human feeling. The maternal sufferings of Constance profoundly move the sympathies and warm the heart, but what are the sensations excited by the remorse and agony of Phædre? We hear a great deal about art for art's sake, and sometimes there is art which delights us simply as art; but the moment you touch human passion art becomes a vehicle only—it ceases to be its own end; it influences character and conduct, and hence you can no more exclude from it questions of morals than you can exclude questions of air from considerations of health. But do not think that I advocate didactic literature. Far from it. The world has been preached to enough—I half suspect, indeed, that excessive sermonizing is the reason why it is so wicked. I view this subject not from the attitude of a professional moralist—one who would fain make all art and literature a vehicle for enforcing moral lessons—but as a man of the world who sees what must inevitably be the influence of a literature that trenches upon dangerous themes. I declare that to speak upon these themes is to utter too much; but I concede that art and literature are moral enough when they avoid topics that are in themselves immoral, their purpose not being didactic. But we have in the studios the same cant about morals in painting and sculpture, especially as expressed in the nude, as we have from the fleshly school of poets and romancists.

Quiver. Do you condemn the delineation of the human figure? I did not suppose you such a Philistine.

Bluff. I am a Philistine, or whatever else you will, to the extent of refusing to be cheated by rant and cant. I claim the human privilege, sir, of examining the ground that theories stand upon. I resent, sir, your application of that word to me. A Philistine is one whom artists and poets cover with immense scorn; but what is a Philistine? Anybody apparently who does not assent to all the notions and wild theories that obtain in the studios and in the Bohemian circles of the beer-gardens. To take a literary view of art—which means, I believe, to judge of a picture by its motive and story rather than by its *technique*—is to be a Philistine; to assume that art and poetry are not the highest things

in life is to utter rank Philistinism; to intimate
that morality should be a force and a factor in art
is to show one's self wholly incapable of discerning
the high purpose of æsthetics, and as a consequence
to merit being cast into the darkness and dreariness
of Philistinism for ever. Let me tell you that this
word Philistinism has become rather too much of a
bugbear. It is used in altogether too arrogant a
fashion by art and literary folk; many people, indeed, seem to be frightened at it, in a very vague
and apprehensive way—pretty much, I fancy, as the
market-woman, in the oft-quoted anecdote, burst into
tears upon being called an hypotenuse. And in
nothing is the dictum of the studios so arrogant as
in the question of nudity in art. It is not only
proper, it is declared, to depict the human figure as
"God made it," but he who shrinks from displays
of this kind, who questions their righteousness, who
believes or fears that they do not exercise a good
influence upon the imaginations of impressible people, is not only a Philistine, but a prurient one; he is
a person whose carnal tendencies have not been
chastened and purified in the high atmosphere of
the Bohemian attic. Now, sir, I am very willing,
indeed, to accept the opinion of the studios upon
any mere art question. The judgment of artists as
to the execution of Page's "Venus," or Powers's

"Greek Slave," is entitled to the greatest respect; but as to the effect upon the popular imagination of these and similar productions I see no reason why I and others are not as good judges as professional men anywhere. And, taking human nature as it is, I do not believe that nude art is anything but pernicious. "To the pure all things are pure," you say; but we are not pure: we have many very powerful passions and evil tendencies; and life and society must be so adjusted that these passions and tendencies are not unnecessarily strengthened.

Quiver. The nude human figure, male or female, in the judgment of innumerable conscientious and excellent persons, is not only a fit subject for art, but is the noblest and most elevating of all subjects that art can treat. In the language of an English writer, to say that "the crown and glory of creation is an improper subject for art is to accuse the Creator of obscenity."

Bluff. Then, sir, by a parallel argument, we accuse the Creator of obscenity when we cover up his handiwork with clothing, and declare it immodest to reveal it. We have only, sir, to glance at the past of mankind to see that in all ages and in all countries the instinct of every people has been to drape and conceal the person. Even the rudest savages make some slight attempt to cover up their nakedness, while every race as it emerges from savagery indicates its progress by its multiplication of apparel. There is no state of nature in which human beings are wholly unconscious of nakedness, animals alone enjoying this lofty superiority to evil. That which was originally an instinct has been strengthened by custom, until clothes have become almost our second selves. Hawthorne, being much wearied and even disgusted with the excessive nudity in art everywhere in Rome, affirmed that in our developed civilization we are fairly born with our clothes on. It is certain that the human race, civilized or half civilized, is now known only in its habiliments. Everywhere men and women protect and conceal their bodies and limbs, guarding their persons with watchful care as something sacred to themselves. There are and have been some modifications of this principle, but modesty has always essentially been looked upon as one of the first of the virtues. From the earliest infancy this principle is instilled — from childhood every rightly trained person is taught to respect, to hold apart, to veil this " crown and glory of creation." How is it, then, that that which is so reverently covered up in actual life may be so fully revealed in art ? How is it that, if

> " The chariest maiden is prodigal enough
> If she unmask her beauty to the moon,"

that maiden beauty may be unmasked in painting
and sculpture for all the world to look upon with
unconsciousness, without a blush, without a suspi-
cion that it is wrong?

Quiver. You are confounding nature and art.

Bluff. They can not be separated in such a question as this. Instinct and education unite in declaring that if nudity is inadmissible in life it must be
inadmissible in all forms of imitation. Every modest person looks at first, I am convinced, upon nude
art with shrinking and inward questioning; and it is
only by a train of artificial reason, by a suppression
of instincts and natural impulses, that he teaches
himself to think it permissible. Civilization has
made a mystery of the person, whether wisely or
not, and it is simply impossible for art to uncover
this mystery without grave consequences. Art, moreover, is never content with depicting the female figure simply and severely, but idealizes it on the side
of voluptuous beauty, enriches it with every fascination of line and tint, carves it with every elaboration
of skill, in order that it may appeal distinctly to the
senses and the emotions. Realistic nude art would
often be disenchanting enough, but what nude art is
there that is not purposely made seductive, that is
not intended to fascinate and allure? It is asserted
that familiarity with the human figure in art would

deaden sexual impressibility to it; but this it is not easy to prove or deny. Art is prolific and free among certain peoples notoriously inflammable; but, while some may believe that nude art has not stimulated passion in these communities, it is obvious that it has not been restrained by making the human form familiar.

Quiver. In some form I admit that nude art may be hurtful. The delineation of a nude female figure may be just as the artist proposes—either the embodiment of innocence, or on the other hand suggestive in every feature and line of lewdness.

Bluff. Distinctly lewd statues and paintings, sir, commonly furnish their own antidote, for they excite nothing but disgust in the mind of every spectator not hopelessly depraved. It is the subtile fascinations of productions not intentionally lewd that allure and stimulate the imagination.

Quiver. Every person should so educate himself as not to be affected in this way.

Bluff. Here, sir, you concede the whole point at issue: the man of the world schools himself to look upon all exhibitions of the kind with critical coolness; he holds his susceptibilities well under control; but this fact establishes the truth of all I have said. Paintings and statues are not made for men of the world, but for the whole race—for susceptible and inflammatory youth as well as for trained connoisseurs. Sexual passion is implanted in all healthy natures; and it is in the young a powerful and dangerous force, which it is necessary to keep under subjection, and in order to do this it is wise to avoid temptation in every form. It must be remembered—what artists, perhaps, do not fully realize—that the attitude of cursory observers toward nude art is very different from their own. It is declared that it is impossible to learn to draw the draped figure accurately without a knowledge of the conformation beneath. This being true, life-schools are necessary, and it is easy to see how pupils at these schools may draw from models without falling under the influences which nude art exercises in public galleries. The artist here is on common ground with the surgeon or physician in many delicate duties, when an important and special purpose dominates all other ideas. The student is delighted with the admirable lines and curves of the human figure; he is struggling to master the difficulties of form and expression, and hence his attitude is wholly academic. But he is in error when he assumes that this academic relation to art does or can exist generally among laymen. The feelings that a beautiful form excites in the artist are certain to be different from those which spring up in the breast of the ordinary observer, who is sure not to be occupied with questions of execution or artistic scholarship, but with the emotions which take possession of him.

Quiver. Your sentiments, sir, are calculated to be resented by a large class. There are persons even who claim for art, in its privilege to display the human form in unconcealed dignity and charm, an agency of spiritual culture—to open, quoting a writer on this theme, "the insight to that mystical unity of the spiritual, intellectual, and sensuous elements of our nature."

Bluff. All of which I do not and can not understand. How spiritual culture is to be furthered by sensuous delineations of physical beauty, by the alluring fascinations of Venuses and Junos, it is hard to say—but this, of course, is because I am wholly carnal-minded. I might point out that Venus, the goddess of beauty, is the most frequently chosen subject for delineation, and this distinctly because she is the ideal of voluptuous female beauty, but I would only be scoffed at. And yet it is the fact that not one nude work of art in a hundred has any thought of spiritual beauty or intellectual beauty, or springs from any desire to glorify the human body, but all are solely and wholly conceived and executed as portraits of physical, sensuous beauty, rarely as something ethereal, spiritual, or divine — of which

some writers say so much. No, sir, the whole thing
is obvious enough. The human figure is clothed by
the necessities of climate as well as by the dictates
of modesty; and a mystery thereby is made of the
body which art can not unfold to curious speculation without danger. The imagination of youth
speedily catches fire at the vision of female beauty
that art reveals; it finds no fascination in coarse,
lewd art, but a world of untold and dangerous emotions in the loveliness that sculptor and painter delight to dwell upon—more distinctly in painting than
in sculpture, no doubt, the latter being necessarily
more severe, on account of its lack of color. To
say that youthful imagination ought not to be sen-
suously stirred by art of this kind is to require of it
more than is possible in nature. Such emotions are
natural, but they are dangerous because they are apt
to lead to great evil, and consequently the moralists
are right in deploring all art and literature that tend
to inflame them. The plain common-sense of the
world is right in this thing, as it is in many other
things which philosophers and critics quarrel over.

XV

MR. BLUFF AS A CRITIC ON DRESS.

(*On the Veranda.*)

MIRANDA,
BACHELOR BLUFF.

"VERY charming indeed, Miss Miranda, and very picturesque."

"I am glad you like it," exclaimed Miranda, her face flushing with pleasure at the Bachelor's praise of her new attire.

"There is certainly," said Mr. Bluff, "a very noticeable revival of the picturesque in ladies' apparel. Your Gainsborough hat, now, with its broken, artistic sweep, its broad brim that shadows the face so charmingly, gives an indescribable piquancy to your expression; and then your gown—is it not a Dolly Varden?—is bewitchingly pert and audacious. Fashion does not often permit women to be so charming."

"I don't see how you can say that, sir. Every fashion is charming when it is in vogue."

"What! are there no principles of taste, no laws of combination? How can putting a thing in vogue make it handsome, or putting it out of vogue make it unhandsome?"

"But just see, sir, how ugly old fashions seem to us now; they didn't look so queer and outlandish when they were the style."

"Nevertheless, they must in fact have been just as queer and outlandish. Use familiarized us to them; and use has doubtless the power to blind us to deformity by gradually deadening our sensibilities. A truly good 'style,' as you call it, can never appear worse than what it is. The real test of the beauty of a costume is its effect upon us when it is not in fashion. No truly good costume, no dress built up upon correct artistic principles, can possibly do anything else than affect us pleasantly, first and last. Greek drapery, a Corinthian capital, or a Greek statue, fills us with delight always. The measure of our pleasure will increase as our knowledge enlarges and our tastes become refined, but pure beauty never has to vindicate itself; it compels admiration in all countries and in all ages. A person often appears ridiculous when dressed up in old bygone toggery, but this is never the case when the toggery is of really good character. We may laugh at a young girl disguised as Aunt Hannah, with pillow-sleeves, a 'poke' bonnet, and her waist at her arm-pits; but we could find nothing to laugh at if the same young girl should appear before us costumed as a Greek vestal. It is not time, nor age, nor familiarity, young lady, that makes a given style of dress ugly or handsome, but the presence or absence of art principles."

"Really, Mr. Bluff, you are not pretending to know anything about ladies' dresses!"

"A very little; but one may get an idea or two by making comparisons. But am I not right? Did you ever turn over a book of costumes, and observe the succession of frightful fashions that have been in vogue at different times? and have you not quickly seen the reason why they are frightful — that it is because fantastic caprice and not laws of taste have governed them? Do you know that in the serious drama it would be simply impossible in many cases for an actress to appear before a modern audience dressed with absolute historic accuracy? This can be done commonly in cases where queenly robes are worn; in almost all other instances a costume strictly correct would excite the risibilities of the spectators, and turn the tragedy into a comedy. Imagine a seri-ous play of the time of the First Empire, with the heroine in scant skirts, just reaching to her boot-tops, with her waist under her arm-pits, and a coiffure towering to the skies ! Such a heroine might be very amusing in an eccentric comedy, but would appear ridiculous in exhibitions of intense feeling. No actress in the world dares to costume herself in all her parts with historic accuracy; she is compelled to modify, and adapt, and as far as possible introduce changes based on correct principles."

"How strange it is," said Miranda, "that often, when we see old portraits of women celebrated in their time for their beauty, it is impossible to see any beauty at all ! They just look horrible, with their frightful head - dresses, and queer laces, and *outré* gowns."

"Those old ugly fashions lost, no doubt, much of their ugliness through familiarity, but women sometimes succeeded in maintaining grace and beauty despite the extraordinary pains that were taken to extinguish those qualities. The native charms of the wearer, the flashing eye, the rising color of the cheek, the dazzling smile, the fascination of manner and voice—things which disappear from the painted image—all these were there to charm, to captivate, and to partially overcome the great drawback of a preposterous get-up—to use a phrase of the green-room. It must have been some hideous style in vogue at the time that prompted the poet to declare that lovely woman unadorned is adorned the most. In all ages men have made their vehement protests against the ugly and fantastic decrees of fashion, but in all ages men, notwithstanding the deformities of mistaken art, have admired the loveliness of women so far as it has survived devices to obliterate it."

" What would you have us do, Mr. Bluff, in order to prevent ugly styles coming into fashion ? "

" Do not surrender yourself so unreservedly to every new device of the mantua-makers, and learn a· few elementary principles of taste. You study a little the harmonies of colors, but you give no heed to the principles of lines and proportion. Nature understood her business when she placed the waist of the human figure where it is ; but tailors and *modistes* are continually trying to make a new law of proportion—at one time by thrusting the waist half-way up to the shoulders, at another by extending it down over the hips—and you ignorantly permit them to play these tricks without rebuke or reproach. It is impossible for a hat to look becoming and graceful if it does not follow the lines of the head, and throw the face partly in shadow.

11

But you wear your hat at one time perched on your nose, at another on the back of your neck, at another you set it up on a mountain of hair. In all these things you evince no sense of fitness, of harmony of form, of the law of subordination of parts. You want everything equally conspicuous. One of the greatest defects in your attire is an excess of trimming—a taste which in its origin is purely barbaric. Why do you hang ribbons, and flowers, and bugles, and laces, and trinkets, and gewgaws of endless kinds all over your gowns? All this is abominable, and most offensive to an instructed eye. A fresh, natural flower in your hair or at your waist is exquisite; but a great array of artificial flowers in your bonnet, at your neck, running up and down your gowns, is something that certainly is not pleasing, nor artistic, nor becoming, nor even civilized. An over-trimmed garment is fussy and frivolous; it lacks dignity; it has no repose; it gives no sense of beauty; it is petty, paltry, senseless, meaningless, and vulgar. A woman's drapery should be rich and quiet; it should fall in ample, graceful folds; it should depend for its beauty on the material and the color, and not on foreign ornaments crowded upon it. The art and the beauty of simplicity ladies either do not understand, or else they permit themselves to be ruled absolutely at the dictation of their *modistes.* But perhaps it is fortunate that they do blunder in this way."

" How so ? "

" If lovely woman knew perfectly well how to adorn herself, how to heighten her beauty, how to set off her charms to their best advantage, it would go hard with the men. It is difficult, as it is, to resist the fascinations of your sex; if, then, you should bring in perfect art to your aid; if your toilets were always perfect studies, the whole masculine world would be at your feet: there is no heart so obdurate that it could resist you."

" You are satirical, sir."

" No, upon my honor, I am not."

" You do not speak of the want of taste in men's apparel. You certainly do not think your sex superior to ours in this particular."

" Men are not expected to have taste. The styles worn by them have often been abominable enough, but we must really yield to your sex the palm for ingenious ugliness in the way of attire. But tailors as well as *modistes* rule. The classical model of manly beauty requires broad shoulders and narrow hips, and yet the time has been when fashion dogmatically declared that the coats of men should be padded at the hips and the lines converge at the neck. Men's coats do not narrow at the shoulder now, but they

are commonly made wide at the hip, in direct violation of the fundamental law. And then see how our
hatters continually make hat-brims at right angles
with the face! Nature never makes a right angle,
abhors right angles, but hatters set up a law to
themselves, and continue to make themselves and
others believe that a stiff, uncurved line around the
head is the right thing."

"I wonder why men care for such things?" said
Miranda. "No one likes to see a handsomely
dressed man. It is foppish and unmanly."

"And yet, by the laws of Nature, men should be
adorned and decorated instead of women."

"What next? Be so good as to explain this
notion."

"Is it not true that nearly all through the animal
species the male is more splendid than the female?
The barn-yard cock struts in brilliant crest and
feathers, while the hen, in more quiet tints, moves
about demure, simple, modest, content to act its little domestic part, and leave pomp and beauty to its
master. The peacock's beauty and vanity are notorious; and how marked they are beside the quiet,
gray peahen! The marvelous plumage of the bird-
of-paradise adorns the male alone; the stag tosses
his superb antlers proudly in the air, while the
doe stands modest and shrinking at his side; the

majestic mane of the lion belongs only to the masculine sex. In some cases the difference between the male and the female is very slight, but, whenever there is a difference, it is invariably, I believe, in favor of the male. In man the beard supplies the natural distinction seen in almost every species."

"Are you going to argue, Mr. Bluff," asked Miranda, with great disdain, "that it is the province of man to wear splendid colors?"

"I am only asking how it is that in the human species all this adornment and splendor have been transferred to the female? How is it that art has been permitted to step in, and seemingly to reverse a principle of creation?"

"I am sure I do not know," said Miranda.

"Let us see if we can not discover the reason. The distinction between the sexes that we are considering is largely due, according to Darwin, to the admiration of the female animal for beauty of color and splendor of form. The female bird, for instance, usually so gray and quiet of feather, so modest and simple in its own demeanor, is delighted with the bright crests and brilliant plumes of its male attendants, and selects for its mate among its admirers him of the gayest feather. While the male is the most brilliantly adorned, it is the female, observe, for

whom this adornment exists—it is the female whose
eye is pleased, whose instincts are gratified in the
beauty of its mate. Do you see where this argument will lead us? Women, who adorn themselves
in such splendid robes, who exhibit such keen appreciation of color and ornament and beauty, are
simply transferring to their own persons those qualities for which they primarily have an intense admiration, but which in Nature are displayed for the
delight of females in individuals of the opposite sex.
It is something of a usurpation on your part, it must
be confessed, this decking yourselves for your own
admiration, but our sex has, very generally, cheerfully
surrendered to you this privilege. Perhaps you will
say that, as males have ceased to be handsome and
brilliant, your natural tastes must have some sort of
vent; that, not having a chance to admire the picturesque in men, you must produce it in yourselves
for your own gratification. Satisfy your conscience in
any way you can ; the argument, at least, shows that
you came naturally by your love of gay apparel, and
that is something."

"If we come naturally by it," said Miranda, "we
are the best judges of it; we have the instinct, the
inborn taste, the natural rightful perceptions; and
you have only a set of crabbed, perverse, cold-blood-
ed notions."

" But, in Nature, colors are never mixed inharmoniously, and there are fitness and purpose in everything. As your tastes come from Nature, study Nature so as to get at her ways of doing things, and then you will silence criticism, and win unqualified admiration from us all. There has been an immense improvement in recent years in home art: many books have been written to aid people in decorating their walls and selecting their furniture; artists of repute even have not thought it beneath them to design wall-papers and cabinet-ware; but no apostle has arisen in the name of artistic dress. It is true that we hear of some attempts in London to revive Greek drapery for women, and there is a clique known by the newly coined word ' æsthetes,' that affect mediæval eccentricities in dress and ecstatic eccentricities in manner; but I am not aware of any distinct attention, wise or unwise, being given to the subject here. In fact, artists, so far from concerning themselves about dress, are perhaps the worst-dressed men in the community—or, if they do consider dress, they put on a general air of dilapidation, as if slovenliness and disorder are indispensable to the picturesque. But let men be ill dressed if they will, it is woman that all men delight in seeing beautifully garbed. Dress richly, dress with splendor, dress with every device that will enhance your beauty, but remember my injunction, that really good dressing must be founded on artistic principles, and not on caprice."

" I would rather be out of the world," exclaimed Miranda, with spirit, " than out of fashion."

XVI

MR. BLUFF DISCUSSES SUNDRY TOPICS.

(At the Club.)

[Upon a summer evening, Bachelor Bluff sat at the club by an open window, lingering over a claret-cup, and chatting with three or four who . had gathered around him. The conversation was very discursive, wandering hither and thither, touching upon many themes, and falling into different moods. It lasted into the small hours of the morning, the stillness of the street and the growing coolness seeming to exercise a pleasing spell upon the garrulous talker and his listeners. The Chronicler gathered up a few fragments of the varied discussion, which are here presented.]

—— " *Great thinkers!* Philosophers, men of science, economists, jurists, are often great thinkers, but poets and men of letters rarely. Poets deal with sentiments and images, and essayists are commonly nothing more than rhetoricians. What is great thinking? It is separating complex phenomena and discovering the truth that underlies them. A man is not a great thinker because he is master of a picturesque and stirring literary style, or because he has something original and striking to say about many subjects, or because he has unusual power of presentation. Great thinking means penetrative and accurate thinking, thinking that establishes truths and fixes principles, that solves problems, that enables us to understand ourselves and thereby to adjust our relations to things around us, that separates fact from speculation and error from falsehood. Great thinkers, you see, are few by this rule; and your Carlyles, Hugos, and Emersons, who are continually held up as thinkers, are far from being really such. They are simply men with a notable capacity for uttering sounding generalities—and generalities that are as often sophistries as anything else. Carlyle, with whose name the world has lately been ringing, was a phrase-maker, and very much more concerned with the effect of what he said than with the truth of what he said."

"I really must challenge you there," said a listener. "Carlyle, I should say, was preëminently a lover of truth."

"He had a great disdain for falsehood, and he

admired sturdy self-assertion; but that nice sense
which strives to analyze accurately and express with
careful precision, he did not possess. He indulged
to great excess in the artist's exaggeration: he is the
rhetorician always, first and last. He possessed a
copious and unique vocabulary; his sentences are
quaint, rugged, and eminently picturesque; he has a
grim humor that gives a ripe flavor to many passages,
and a power of trenchant imprecation that is fairly
unapproachable. These qualities make his writings
in their way superb. One gets new ways of looking
at familiar things, he is entertained by striking and
admirable utterances, his ear tingles with a splendid
but barbaric resonance; and all this turbulence,
these bustling and strangely discordant sentences,
this rude force and grotesque decoration, this profusion of strange ideas and stranger words, all seem
no doubt indeed very like wonderful thinking. But
what ideas has he given to the world? He is a
fierce denouncer of shams, and a passionate lover
of force. He admires earnest truthfulness, the spirit
of loyalty, and self-abnegation. He storms at ve-
nality, at feebleness, at selfishness, at pretension, at
crookedness of all kinds, at all ignoble and demean-
ing things — but while all this is of good service,
especially when uttered with authority and force, it
does not constitute great thinking. A vehement

passion for worth and an aptitude for picturesque
scolding may be rightly entitled to praise, but one
does not come thereby to understand life and the
world any better. This temper does not throw light
on dark places; nor indicate the means whereby the
evils of society may be abated or reformed; nor aid
us in adjusting conditions, making laws, or administering affairs. The unhappy world that from the
beginning has stumbled on through slough and mo-
rass, hoping for and struggling toward the light,
must go on in its desperate endeavor, utterly unaided by anything that Carlyle did or said. Did I
say unaided? Will it not rather have been obstructed and defeated? It has gathered some comfort from a voice that has sounded for honesty and
uprightness, but for the most part this voice has
mocked it; for Carlyle detested the growth of freedom, clamored for the restoration of force and authority, preached to men but one virtue, submission
—his whole philosophy being, roughly, ' Grin and
bear it.' These are very good words at times, and
under right circumstances; but who is this thinker,
this prophet, who can not understand that mankind
have aspirations and hopes, who comes only to denounce and never to cheer, who imagines that servile submission and not independent effort gives
greatness to the race?"

——— "Yes! I like a good play, and I like the new actors so long as they confine themselves to modern plays. A new style of composition has come up, and new methods of acting. Our actors have lost a good deal and learned a good deal; and in their own particular fashion I accept them cordially. In parlor plays, in the realistic emotional drama, in the light, sweet comedies of the Robertson school, the new people are very agreeable; they have learned how to be colloquial, they have caught the manners of society, they know how to be earnest and simple, and they have banished from the stage a good many of its tricks and affectations. I like them very well, indeed; but they must let the old comedy alone—it overwhelms them completely. The broad method, the rich unction, the audacious effects, the ripe, mellow tone, like the *impasto* of the old painters— these are all gone. Two or three old parts linger on the stage in the hands of the last representatives of the old school, but when these men leave us a distinct art will utterly disappear. Even brilliant high comedy is gone. There are no more Mirabels, Young Rovers, Charles Surfaces, Benedicks; the splendid art of the old actors in these parts, their captivating gayety, their superb *aplomb*, the dazzling rattle of their spirits—the world has lost it all. It is a great change, and a change that no one can realize who has never seen any of the old personations. The new people are very effective in their way; and I suspect the old actors would be as ill at ease in the new parlor comedy as their successors are when they try to fill out a Sir Anthony Absolute or a Dr. Ollapod. But there is one loss that can not be compensated for—this is the art of speaking. None of the new actors know how to talk. I saw a Shakespearean play recently, and there was but one man on the stage that knew how to speak a line. Anybody can utter the colloquial commonplaces of the later comedy, wherein the art is almost wholly in what one *does*, not in what he *says;* but elocution is a lost art. It is true, a whole army of elocutionists have been let loose upon us; they abound, I suppose, on the principle that doctors multiply in sickly places. But these elocutionists know little of true elocution; they are mimics, dialect - speakers, plat-form-actors, face-makers, declaimers, what-not; but of that exquisite art which throws radiance on a poetic line, bringing out its complete meaning and full expression—this art is guessed at a little, but not at all understood. Charlotte Cushman had it; Ellen Tree had it marvelously; Edwin Forrest, with all his defects, and a disposition to play with syllables, was not without it; and Edwin Booth, with all his many fine qualities, has it not—for his utterance is monotonous and hard, and lacks the illuminating touches that made the old delivery so delightful. Well, the art has gone, the army of elocutionists to the contrary, as they may; but I like good acting of the kind we have very well indeed — yet not in Shakespeare, not in the old comedy."

" Does not the difference between these two styles of acting indicate the change that has come over the time ? "

" Undoubtedly. It has been said, when speaking of our great-grandfathers, that those who drank port-wine thought port-wine. Certainly, a rich, crusty flavor—a mellow, broad heartiness—that characterized the last century, has disappeared ; and there is substituted instead a very thin, acrid form of humanity, which, to the generous unction of the old time, is what claret is to port. The spirit of the old comedy was its hearty, almost boisterous, mirth, its supreme and untroubled gayety. As distinguished from this, the merriest humors of the new comedy are partially cynical; if there is a laugh, it is the laugh of satiety, of the *blasé ;* or, at best, the mirth is that of the philosopher who, discovering the vanity of all things, is merry with a sort of pitiful disdain. Our latest comedy, moreover, is reticent and repressive ; it has the repose of the Vere de Veres; it is nonchalant, indifferent, epicurean. Its motto is

'*Nil admirari.*' Its love-making and its heroism
are alike both cool and slightly scornful. It reflects accurately certain tendencies of the age; and,
just as we find no rollicking mirth, no abounding
spirits, no ripe and eager zest in the heroes of the
mock life before the foot-lights, neither do we find
them in the real life of the men and women around
us. Mirabel, or Rover, or Doricourt, with their
huge exhilaration, their glorious spirits, their superb
animality, are possible only in a past existence and
a past art. We have all turned speculators and
thinkers, students and economists. We are indifferent to almost everything but the spirit of criticism;
we are fastidious, cynical, hypercritical; we affect
taste, and yet our manners are as negative as our
spirits, and we have utterly outgrown the magnificent suavity of the old school. We may well sometimes wish that our modern life could catch a little
of the warmth and lusty *abandon* of a hundred years
ago; but it can not be. Each age has unchange-
ably its own characteristics."

——— " The gift to see ourselves as others see us !
My good sir, that would be an uncomfortable talisman for most of us. Without a little self-delusion
in this particular, life would scarcely be tolerable.
No, sir, that is not the gift, despite Mr. Poet Burns,

that we need or could well endure; but, now, if some one would endow us with the gift of seeing things as other people see them, that would be a boon. It would multiply sensations, increase the number of our ideas, fairly enlarge the boundaries of life. Gentlemen, I am a little in love with my own fancy; I imagine one in possession of the power of entering into the intelligence of other people, by the aid of some sprite having the faculty of translating himself into the identity of each person he meets— of coiling himself up, as it were, in the imagination of a poet, and seeing with his ravished eyes the beauties of the world; of gliding into the fancies of a man of science and penetrating with him the mysteries of nature; of entering with passionate delight into an artist's studies of the hills and woods; into the speculations of statesmen, and seeing how states are ruled; into the schemes of the man of business whose projects people the wilderness and reach to the antipodes; into the sports and gay pleasures of youth; into a lover's ecstasy; into an old man's tender recollections of pleasures gone by—seeing, briefly, life on all its sides, things in all their aspects. This would be a better gift than the purse of Fortunatus."

—— "Well, sir, as to another World's Fair, why, with all my heart; but this time let it be a Fair

showing what has *not* been done, which of all the nations has shown most skill in the art of *not* doing.
Such an exhibition would be something new, and
likely to do as much good as anything yet of the
kind, although the world might not be very proud
of it. An exhibit of how badly a city can be governed would be very appropriate, such as a section
of metropolitan pavement, an example of a neglected
wharf, a model of an unrepressed dram-shop, an interior of a splendid gambling palace, a vivid picture
of a nine-story tenement-house swarming with degraded women and ragged children, a dramatic rep-
resentation showing how justice is administered in
police courts. New York, of course, should send
this contribution, and she would be sure of a medal.
The General Government might send a specimen of
how officials are appointed, with a model of a mis-
placed consul, and one of a regulation custom-house
officer. Each political party should send a diagram
illustrating how the wrong man gets nominated for
office. The railroad companies should send a first-
class example of the discomforts of American railway-
traveling, illustrating passengers suffocated with dust,
persecuted with pop-corn peddlers, and fastened down
in narrow, hard, and inquisitorial seats. A model
of a soiled railway-station would be proper, with to-
bacco-spitters and peanut-eaters in the waiting-rooms,

and dirt and *débris* heaped around it. Another edifying exhibit would be a railway-train crashing through a bridge, or tumbling over a cliff. A choice specimen of a summer barrack, called a summer hotel, should be there, with every detail of the annoyance it implies faithfully depicted. Care would need to be taken to represent the average American highway, the average American suburban villa, the crowded American horse-car, the politeness of officials everywhere, the urbane car-conductor— But I must stop. Do not expect me to give you a whole catalogue ; I have said enough for you to see that, if rightly carried out, an exhibition on this plan would be a great but most uncomfortable success."

—— " What a really magnificent city New York might become if the people were only inspired with the intense local pride that once animated the citizens of Athens, of Rome, of Venice, or of the great free cities of Germany ! Its situation, in some particulars, is wonderfully fine, but, while everybody acknowledges this fact, it is not fully comprehended. That the city lies near the sea, with a splendid bay at its foot, and is washed on each side by a noble river, is perceived ; but in what way have these facts been turned to account ? For anything one may see as he walks the streets, New York might be an in-

land city, standing in an arid plain. The splendid
waters that surround it bestow no convenience, no
beauty, no features of health, recreation, or attrac-
tion. Resting upon an inlet of the sea, it has superb outlooks, but they are given over to dirt and
disorder, it being the inscrutable law of cities that
refuse and loafers shall ever drift down to the water's edge. There is a Battery that commands a bay
which for beauty is excelled by but one or two in
the world, and for picturesque animation is unequaled. But the Battery is given over to immigrants,
who alone enjoy the fresh sea air and the varied panorama—our citizens, for the most part, turning their backs upon it; and yet what a place for a
terrace, for a belvedere, for grand baths, for marble
walks and classic gardens, for some great display of
architectural beauty! No city in the world has a
spot so fitted for the exercise of the architect's or
gardener's skill. The broad bay, the green hills
that encompass it, the tossing waters, the anchored
ships, the swift steamboats that come and go, the immense stir and life—all make up a fascinating picture, but it is surrendered to stragglers and strangers.
There ought to be erected a lofty tower with a look-
out, or hanging gardens—some unique architectural
structure, to which citizens might resort for rest, sea-
air, and an opportunity to look upon the unsur-

passed picture always to be found there. There should also be erected baths—I do not mean swimming-barracks—but structures of marble such as would vie with the famous baths of old Rome. And then look at the rivers that border the city! Why should the whole stretch of their shores be given exclusively to wharves and trade? Here and there an embankment or a belvedere should be erected, to which the people could resort on summer days and evenings and inhale the fresh air. Were there such things in the hearts of the people as a passion for art, a taste for the grand, the water boundaries of New York would present a succession of noble piers for commerce, superb baths for health, splendid belvederes and river-side gardens, such as would give grace and beauty to its shores and make the city famous. But you are saying to yourselves, ' This is the dream of a visionary.' Let me tell you that it is only by exalted conceptions of the kind that cities become great. Neither Babylon nor Rome became the wonder of the world save by high ambition and lofty local pride. Sloth, indolence, indifference, low tastes and desires, never did and never will give largeness and dignity to the habitations of men."

—— " How great is the stir and commotion of the times ! The many-sided elements that make up

our population remind me at times of that vivid
era in ancient history when Italians and Greeks,
Egyptians and Jews, Goths and Germans, Numidi-
ans and Britons, Christians and pagans, were united
under the dominion of the Roman eagle—when from
the Atlantic to the Euphrates, from Sahara to the
forests of Germany, turbulent and active millions of
widely different nationalities and habits jostled each
other in half-amicable contention, and filled the world
with the stir and bustle of their doings. In America
we have now as varied nationalities and as contrasted social elements. The four quarters of the globe
are with us cheek by jowl; Africans and Mongoli-
ans, Teutons and Celts, Gauls and Saxons, Jews and
Egyptians, Indians and Asiatics, Slavs and Italians
—people of all nationalities unite under the ægis
of our flag, vastly heterogeneous under our freedom
for individual development, but swiftly acquiring
a measure of homogeneity by reason of liberalizing
intercourse. These national diversities are supplemented by local diversities, and these again are varied by the perfect opportunity for individual action;
and so everywhere we see strange differences and
yet unity—the struggle and friction of elements that
by nature oppose and contend, and which yet by
law and national pressure are abraded into certain
unities of purpose. All these contrasted and con-

tending features produce throughout the country a
picturesque turbulence that recalls the commotion
of Rome, Constantinople, or Alexandria. The political liberty which brings all sorts of people from
foreign shores is attended by that social liberty
which gives license to all sorts of individual caprice,
and as a result we have a life full of contrast, activity, and collision—a life exuberant, loud, and expan-
sive, which may possibly lack claim to high refinement, but which yet compensates for this by its
lustiness, its courage, and its achievements. In all
our great cities these elements are notably conspicuous; but New York especially seems in a perpetual
flutter of exuberant life. There are here ceaseless
outbursts of the elements that make up its population, constantly the loudest demonstration of different organizations, nationalities, or modes of thought,
while in pleasure as well as in business we are fairly
stunned with the excess of confused activity. The
Germans flaunt their banners and utter their pæans
of triumph to-day; the Irish fill our streets with
rude pageantries to-morrow; and all peoples in
some form express their national feelings. The
drama and opera of every tongue have representatives; the sports of all climes are reproduced in our
pleasure-grounds; and, in our own individual way,
we break out into clamorous conviviality. How ex-

travagantly we dine and lavishly we drink, the hotels bear witness; what bustle and excitement of
pleasure we delight in, our seashore resorts give
evidence. A certain emphasis in our enjoyments is
one of our developing characteristics. In Wall
Street our business is enacted amid the clatter of
champagne-glasses; on the roads our soberest men
of trade repeat the excitement of the race-course.
Our hotels are marvelous caravansaries; our promenades glory in their processions of gay costumes.
In all things there are emphasis and noise. We
repeat the hot, tumultuous life of Rome when the
Roman Empire had gathered all peoples under her
dominion, and marked her boundaries almost by
the limits of civilization."

—— " Logically women are entitled to the suffrage, whether suffrage be either a right or a privilege. If it is a right, one half of the community
possesses it equally with the other half; if it is a
privilege, who bestows it—from what is it derived?
As matters stand, one part of the community gives
it to itself, which is a little presumptuous, to say the
least. Nevertheless, we must, in self-defense, keep
the suffrage from women as long as possible. The
female sex outnumber us in all the Atlantic States
considerably now, and the difference increases; if

we, therefore, allow women to exercise the elective franchise, there is danger that, instead of making them our political equals, they would become our political superiors; they would outvote us at the polls, and we should find them combining to secure their own legislators. They would elect themselves to all the places of profit and honor; they would retaliate for centuries of unfavorable legislation on our part; they would shut up our clubs, make smoking a penal offense, tax bachelors out of existence, and do innumerable things to enslave us. The only way to escape this dire result is to restore at once the balance of the sexes. How to do it is perplexing; but the supremacy of man, the welfare and security of time-honored institutions, all the interests of society, as we understand them, render its accomplishment necessary. The excess is some one hundred and thirty thousand, I believe; and to dispose of this number is a problem that might well tax the ingenuity of the most adroit statesmanship. To put so large a number under restraint would be impossible with the present penitentiary accommodations, and the cost, moreover, would be alarming. It wouldn't do to put them to the sword—such a solution two thousand years ago would have been the most obvious method of cutting the Gordian knot; but in this sentimental era we have qualms

12

and prejudices. The Herod plan applied to all female infants would in time accomplish the result; and Swift's suggestion in regard to Irish infants would also bring about the desired equilibrium, and at the same time utilize the surplus—but baked female baby is not yet one of our recognized dishes. Can any one show us the way out of this difficulty ? "

—— " Radicalism and Conservatism, instead of being really antagonistical, are simply supplemental. The Radical, for instance, discovers that without progressive thought the world would stagnate. He perceives with great clearness how much has been accomplished in every direction—in opinion, in government, in science, in art, in education, in religion, in society — by an emancipation from the traditions of the past, by bold, speculative thought, and by freedom of action. But the Conservative has equally truthful perceptions. He sees that the safety of society depends upon the maintenance of certain checks and safeguards, without which the whole community would rush into chaos and anarchy. The overthrow of established principles, the substitution of everything untried for everything tried, the disregard of all precedents and all experience, the abolition of all subordination and all order — these things, the Conservative clearly realizes, would break up the foundations of society, and bring us all to revolution and ruin. And doubtless they would. It would never do for Radicalism to have its own way altogether; but neither would it do for Conservatism to hold the world in absolute check. Conservatism and Radicalism are, in truth, centripetal and centrifugal social forces, which balance each other and direct the course of the world."

——"I confess that I am a dreamer," said the Bachelor, falling into a meditative mood—"a lover of the Brown Study, in which, as in a mantle, I often wrap myself. There is no painful reaction in the visions engendered by this harmless day-dreaming, as with those which are stimulated by hasheesh or lotus-eating. There are elements of indulgence and relaxation in it, it is true, but in this harsh world it is strange if we can not permit ourselves at least a few idle dreams of happiness, the only form in which to many of us it can ever come. The Brown Study may be indulged in by an open window, by a slow and slumberous fire, "under green leaves," by river or lake shore, by the solemn surge of the sea, and even amid the stir and bustle of busy highways. Its subjects are as various as life, and its requirements are simply a surrender

of the whole mind to its wayward and capricious
courses. All devotees of the Brown Study come
into large fortunes; fall rapturously in love with
tender-hearted women; achieve great successes in
art, literature, or commerce; with princely
munificence exhaustless wealth; create rare Utopias;
turn labor, skill, genius, application, love, and all human sentiments, into triumphant engines of earthly
bliss. Nature bursts into beauty, and art into production; the heavens smile and the winds are tem-
pered; all that the fancy covets, the senses love, or
the heart yearns for, spring into form and life at the
command of this mystic talisman. It deadens pain,
gilds labor, sweetens care, and fills the soul with
soft pleasure. It is one of the fine qualities of the
Brown Study, that its students are endowed with
charity and good-will. The munificence of their gifts,
the breadth and comprehensiveness of their largess,
are noble. In fact, one of the keenest pleasures experienced under the influence of this study, is the
ability which it dreamingly affords of scattering happiness around, whether the reveries be of wealth, or
love, or friendship, or success. This alone ought to
redeem the habit from the charge of idle dreaming.
A bliss that multiplies itself by wide bestowing, a
happiness that discovers a most exquisite delight in
its power to bless, must leave a sweetness in the

heart worth all the indulgence and relaxation by
which it is created. But why has this species of
dreaming received the somber name of Brown? Is
it because it is most often evoked by the brown cigar,
or the smoke-colored pipe? Is there something in
the rapt, lost, far-away look of the dreamer that is
dun and dim, as if the soul had faded away out of
the features, and left them blank and empty? Or
is it because Brown Studies are more frequent in
the autumn of· life, when all things are sere and
somber? Possibly it is because brown is soft and
mellow, and has rich warm depths of character and
expression — and yet brown is of the earth, and
these dreams are tinted with the hues of heaven.
Brown, indeed, the outward aspect may be; but a
delicious dreaming that lights up the soul with
glorious colors, that fills the imagination with pomp
and splendor, that converts all things into beauty,
promise, and delight, should to my notion be entitled a Golden Study."

—— "*Natural justice!* There is no such thing.
If there is natural justice, where and how is it exhibited? In what does it exist? In what way, I
ask, has society supplanted or disregarded it? In
Nature, sirs, there is neither justice, nor equity, nor
equality; there is but one fundamental principle,

and this is might. Throughout the whole dominion
of Nature the lesser is ever conquered and absorbed
by the greater; the weak succumb to the strong,
the big consume the little; life in one form is de-
stroyed to perpetuate life in another form. The
operations of Nature are harsh and inexorable, without mercy, without pity, without any sentiment so-
ever, possessing one sole attribute — that of power.
The equal right of different individuals to life, liberty, and happiness, is unknown. If we derive our
ideas of right and wrong from certain implanted
instincts, we certainly do not find their verification
in any of the aspects of untamed Nature. Justice
has no existence save as an intellectual perception
of cultivated man—it is not a law of Nature, but
the sublime conception of man. How absurd, then,
are all these frequent appeals to natural justice!
The right term is natural injustice; and if we look
closely we will see that this elementary principle is
continually operating in society; that there is always a persistent conflict between natural injustice
and human justice. As in Nature the big consume
the little, so in society we find the strong controlling and absorbing the weak, the lesser contributing
to the fruition of the greater, despite our struggles
to have it otherwise. As society has advanced,
things have changed much more in name than in

fact. Trade is acting in the same way that military prowess did once, building up in the hands of the few enormous power, virtually derived from the subordination of the many: hence now we have Rothschilds and Vanderbilts, instead of Warwicks and Percies. The battle of life is between natural tendencies to power and conquest and human conceptions of right; and, instead of appealing to Nature, it must be our purpose to revoke its order, to disregard its example, if we wish to firmly establish the principle of social justice."

—— " *The age unpoetic and unheroic !* Such are current complaints, I know, but are they true ? Poetry and heroism change some of their aspects from age to age, and it may be that those who lament their decadence are simply failing to discern those virtues under their new guise; but to my mind the age is really neither unpoetic nor unheroic. It is unmistakably a pushing, energetic, money-making age ; it is distinctly an age where practical and utilitarian things have a very high place in the schemes and purposes of the people ; but, notwithstanding all these strong practical activities, there is abundant evidence that poetry and heroism are great existing social forces. The people are eager readers of imaginative literature. They listen not only attentive-

ly to the poets and singers of the time, but they are
manifesting a marked disposition to go back and
study periods of the past.   There are signs of a
revival of classic taste, and the early productions of
literature have now continually increasing hosts of
students and admirers.   While on one hand we see
that realism in art and literature is cultivated, we
also note that higher forms of imaginative thought
lead captive whole ranks of the people.   There
have been more brilliant eras of dramatic and even
of lyric literature, but none in which the poets
have enjoyed so large a body of readers, none in
which they have been permitted so freely to follow
their individual poetic instincts, or have more effectually stirred the popular heart.   Those who look
may see evidence of the truth of what I say on
every hand.   The interest felt in every new production by Tennyson, Longfellow, Lowell, Whittier, Mor-
ris, Swinburne ; the endless essays upon poetry and
the poets in all the magazines—these are substan-
tiating facts.

   " Art also is inspired with both realistic truth
and imaginative force.   Mere story-telling by pictures has declined, but the expression of poetic feeling and sentiment by color and form has taken a
lofty place.   I do not deny that there have been
greater art-epochs, but there is now a marked pas-

sion for studying those epochs; there is an eagerness to be at home with their spirit and to master
their teachings. Mere imitations of ancient methods
are not tolerated, but originality, passion, individual
sentiment, inventive power, are quickly recognized
and applauded. This so-called unpoetic age is com-
pleting in some instances and restoring in others the
great poetical architecture of earlier ages; it is
searching amid the ruins of buried cities for precious art-memorials of the past, and placing the discovered treasures in places of honor; it is bringing
into practical use ancient suggestions in decorative
and ornamental art; it is, in fact, full of reverence
for the great achievements of the imagination that
have come down to it, and is instinct with pleasure
in the stimulating and often daring productions of
to-day. The literature about art is swelling ceaselessly; teachers who instruct what and how to admire are eagerly listened to; and everywhere are the
evidences of how large a place this form of poetic
feeling holds with us.

" And heroism no less than poetry takes its place
in this many-sided era. The loud proclamation and
noisy defiance of some of the earlier forms of heroism do not exist; men now believe it incumbent
upon them to seek no opportunity for the mere display of their gallantry, but also to shrink from no

occasion that exacts fortitude or involves self-sacrifice. That is emphatically not an unheroic age that with so much zeal dares the wilderness of ice in the arctic seas and the wilderness of forest and swamp in the heart of Africa; that delights in conquering hitherto inaccessible mountain-peaks; that penetrates everywhere, explores everywhere, and enters into a multitude of splendid enterprises. Recent wars showed no decline of that physical courage which in earlier ages was so worshiped; and in all the ordinary exigencies of life, fortitude, endurance, the courage to do and to suffer, evince no lack of the true spirit of heroism. You can readily supplement many arguments and facts to those I have advanced, to show that the age has neither lost imaginative sympathy, which is the essential spirit of poetry, nor the fiber of genuine heroism."

—— "Have you noted the recent marked intrusion of the peasant into art and literature, especially French art and literature? Democratic theories and principles are no new things, but genuine democratic sympathies are a development almost of our own time; at least, both art and literature have largely held themselves aloof from phases of lowly life. France once politically deified the people, but that was a spasm of demagogism rather than any genuine

sympathy with the lower classes; but to-day there
are evidences of a new spirit there. A great deal
of recent French fiction is devoted to the delineation and elevation of peasant-life. George Sand,
during the latter part of her life, gave pictures of
rustic and the better forms of peasant life in her
stories almost exclusively. Edmond About gave us
recently, in 'The Story of an Honest Man,' one of
the finest pictures of sturdy, lowly life ever penned;
Theuriet has written some most delightful sketches
of provincial and rustic characters, and set upon a
high place the simple virtues of peasant-life; and
many other French writers have caught up the idea.
But Art, more conspicuously even than Literature,
has opened its arms to this new thought. The
painter Millet, a peasant himself, has revealed the
character, the sorrows, and the struggles of the
peasant to the world; he has challenged its critical
attention and awakened everywhere its sympathies.
The world has long been familiar with the ideal
peasant of the ballet, and the romantic peasant of
the poets, and sometimes caught glimpses in history
of ignorant, brutal, and starved masses; but the real
peasant, just as he is, lowly but human, bent under
many burdens but not without aspirations, has
been effectively delineated only in our own age.
The change that has come over the spirit of art in

this particular betokens the general widening of the
human horizon, the broadening of sympathies, the
coming of that true democracy that shall make the
human family all one brotherhood.   Even a few
decades ago art concerned itself almost solely with
the historic and great.   It thirsted for pomp and
splendor, for great events, for heroes, for ethereal
beauty, for tragic incidents; and now it is turning
from these themes to paint gray skies, uncouth, humble figures, the shadow that lies on the path of the
laborer.   This is a change the philosophy of which
may well be studied."

—— "There is something glorious in youth.   Its
follies never trouble me; I think nothing of its
ignorance when I see its faith and courage; nothing of its vanity and conceit when I see its truth,
its hopeful confidence, its bold aspirations, its passion for splendid dreaming.   Who would not surrender all the acquisitions that have come with time
and take up youth with all its greenness and foolishness, if the Fates offered such a reversion of
life-leases?   By Jove! there would be a precipitate
return to the beautiful days, much as we may affect
to despise them.   Wisdom would fling its learning
down with its gray beard ; Fame would toss its
crown into the air; Power fling its scepter into the

gutter; Greatness rush with more eagerness down
the steps of the temple than it ever ascended them;
and Wealth sweep its coin aside without a murmur
—each taking up the fresh, unworn garment of youth,
and wandering off filled with a rapture known to
our 'green and salad' days only."

—— " There are dull sermons and dull lectures,
no doubt; but there is an almost infallible receipt
for making sermons and lectures interesting."

" What is that, sir?"

" Listen to them. Alert imagination and willing
sympathy are important factors in giving life and
meaning to many things that come before us. What
is wanted in this world more than anything else is
intelligent appreciation; for performance in all the
arts commonly goes beyond the capacity of people
to understand. To the dull all things are dull. No
matter what wealth of color an artist pours upon his
canvas, the picture is meaningless to him who does
not look upon it with quickened apprehension; no
matter with what splendor of imagery a poet adorns
his lines, it is all a babble to him who has no poesy
in his soul. Dante and Shakespeare, Raphael and
Murillo, Beethoven and Handel, all are barren to
the lethargic, insensible mind. Many a line of a
poet has profound significance to a student, which

is but meaningless jargon to the clown ; many a
flower is full of beauty to a naturalist that to the
crude rustic is no more than a worthless weed. As
it is true that

> " ' The ripe flavor of Falernian tides,
>   Not in the wine, but in the taste resides ' ;

as it is certain that the glowing tints of the flower
and the radiant splendors of the sunset depend upon the susceptibility of the retina that mirrors them ;
as it is the delicate sensitiveness in the photographic
plate that catches successfully the shadow of the
sun, and fixes the subtile lines of the image ; as
melody can live only in the attuned ear ; as heat
and light are vital forces only as they act upon the
material substances that receive them — so we may
be assured that the world of mind is equally with
these instances of physical phenomena a matter of
relation and correspondence. No seeds are so fruit-
ful that they can quicken in a desert soil, and few
so feeble that they will not vivify in a generous
loam. In fault-finding criticism, therefore, it is often
uncertain where the defect lies—whether it is really
in the dullness of the producer or in the stubborn
insensibility of the censor."

—— " Fickle Fortune ! It would be good news
to many people if this were true. There are lucky

men to whom Fortune is always faithful, always a
south wind bringing balm and sweet service; and
there are unlucky men to whom she is always
averse, a perpetual east wind, chilling and killing.
Fortune and misfortune in this world are distributed
very much as at a breakfast-table, where all the sugar
is in one vessel and all the mustard in another."

—— "The millennium is not impossible, and not
so very difficult. If every man from this time forth
gave his whole attention to his own sins and vices,
and ceased to make war on other people's sins and
vices, we should have it with the new moon."

—— "A great many people go to church, no
doubt, to honestly confess their sins, but I am
afraid that a larger number go to church to confess their virtues."

—— "Great men, it is often said, are only a
little in advance of the multitude—just as hills and
valleys are alike plunged in darkness at midnight,
but the dawn lightens the hill-tops first."

—— "The cynics will have it that all the world
is selfish, and every son of Adam occupied solely
with himself. The absurdity of this notion is evident

at a glance—for who has not observed the solicitude and concern with which people watch the sins and shortcomings of other people? How anxious they are to bring them to repentance, how pained they are because they are not as wise and virtuous as themselves! Who ever hears a sermon, that he does not generously turn it over to an erring friend; or a wise axiom, that he does not promptly apply it to a sinful enemy? Anxious individuals continually go about lamenting the unfortunate habits and weaknesses of their neighbors, and are in such despair because of the sins and vices of society, that nothing consoles them but the balm of their own virtues."

XVII

MR. BLUFF'S EXPERIENCES OF HOLIDAYS.

Bachelor Bluff,
The Chronicler.

"I HATE holidays," said Bachelor Bluff to me, with some little irritation, on a Christmas a few years ago. Then he paused an instant, after which he resumed: "I don't mean to say that I hate to see people enjoying themselves. But I hate holidays, nevertheless, because to me they are always the dreariest and saddest days of the year. I shudder at the name of holiday. I dread the approach of one, and thank Heaven when it is over. I pass through, on a holiday, the most horrible sensations, the bitterest feelings, the most oppressive melancholy; in fact, I am not myself at holiday-times."

"Very strange," I ventured to interpose.

"A plague on it!" said he, almost with violence. "I'm not inhuman. I don't wish anybody harm. I'm glad people can enjoy themselves. But I hate holidays all the same. You see, this is the reason:

I am a bachelor; I am without kin; I am in a place that did not know me at birth. And so, when holidays come around, there is no place anywhere for me. I have friends, of course; I don't think I've been a very sulky, shut-in, reticent fellow; and there is many a board that has a place for me—but not at Christmas-time. At Christmas, the dinner is a family gathering; and I've no family. There is such a gathering of kindred on this occasion, such a reunion of family folk, that there is no place for a friend, even if the friend be liked. Christmas, with all its kindliness and charity and good-will, is, after all, deuced selfish. Each little set gathers within its own circle; and people like me, with no particular circle, are left in the lurch. So you see, on the day of all the days in the year that my heart pines for good cheer, I'm without an invitation.

"Oh, it's because I pine for good cheer," said the bachelor, sharply, interrupting my attempt to speak, "that I hate holidays. If I were an infernally selfish fellow, I wouldn't hate holidays. I'd go off and have some fun all to myself, somewhere or somehow. But, you see, I hate to be in the dark when all the rest of the world is in light. I hate holidays, because I ought to be merry and happy on holidays, and can't.

"Don't tell me," he cried, stopping the word that was on my lips; "I tell you, I hate holidays. The shops look merry, do they, with their bright toys and their green branches? The pantomime is crowded with merry hearts, is it? The circus and the show are brimful of fun and laughter, are they? Well, they all make me miserable. I haven't any pretty-faced girls or bright-eyed boys to take to the circus or the show, and all the nice girls and fine boys of my acquaintance have their uncles or their grand-dads or their cousins to take them to those places; so, if I go, I must go alone. But I don't go. I can't bear the chill of seeing everybody happy, and knowing myself so lonely and desolate. Confound it, sir, I've too much heart to be happy under such circumstances! I'm too humane, sir! And the result is, I hate holidays. It's miserable to be out, and yet I can't stay at home, for I get thinking of Christmases past. I can't read—the shadow on my heart makes it impossible. I can't walk—for I see nothing but pretty pictures through the bright windows, and happy groups of pleasure-seekers. The fact is, I've nothing to do but to hate holidays.— But will you not dine with me?"

Of course, I had to plead engagement with my own family circle, and I couldn't quite invite Mr. Bluff home *that* day, when Cousin Charles and his

wife, and Sister Susan and her daughter, and three
of my wife's kin, had come in from the country, all
to make a merry Christmas with us. I felt sorry,
but it was quite impossible; so I wished Mr. Bluff
a "merry Christmas," and hurried homeward through
the cold and nipping air.

I did not meet Bachelor Bluff again until a week
after Christmas of the next year, when I learned
some strange particulars of what occurred to him
after our parting on the occasion just described. I
will let Bachelor Bluff tell his adventures for himself:

"I went to church," said he, "and was as sad
there as everywhere else. Of course, the evergreens
were pretty, and the music fine; but all around me
were happy groups of people, who could scarcely
keep down *merry* Christmas long enough to do reverence to *sacred* Christmas. And nobody was alone
but me. Every happy paterfamilias in his pew tan-
talized me, and the whole atmosphere of the place
seemed so much better suited to every one else than
me that I came away hating holidays worse than
ever. Then I went to the play, and sat down in a
box all alone by myself. Everybody seemed on the
best of terms with everybody else, and jokes and
banter passed from one to another with the most
good-natured freedom. Everybody but me was in

a little group of friends. I was the only person in the whole theatre that was alone. And then there was such clapping of hands, and roars of laughter, and shouts of delight at all the fun going on upon the stage, all of which was rendered doubly enjoyable by everybody having somebody with whom to share and interchange the pleasure, that my loneliness got simply unbearable, and I hated holidays infinitely worse than ever.

" By five o'clock the holiday became so intolerable that I said I'd go and get a dinner. The best dinner the town could provide. A sumptuous dinner. A sumptuous dinner for one. A dinner with many courses, with wines of the finest brands, with bright lights, with a cheerful fire, with every condition of comfort—and I'd see if I couldn't for once extract a little pleasure out of a holiday !

" The handsome dining-room at the club looked bright, but it was empty. Who dines at this club on Christmas but lonely bachelors ? There was a flutter of surprise when I ordered a dinner, and the few attendants were, no doubt, glad of something to break the monotony of the hours.

" My dinner was well served. The spacious room looked lonely; but the white, snowy cloths, the rich window - hangings, the warm tints of the walls, the sparkle of the fire in the steel grate, gave the room an air of elegance and cheerfulness; and then the table at which I dined was close to the window, and through the partly-drawn curtains were visible pictures of lonely, cold streets, with bright lights from many a window, it is true, but there was a storm, and snow began whirling through the street. I let my imagination paint the streets as cold and dreary as it would, just to extract a little pleasure by way of contrast from the brilliant room of which I was apparently sole master.

"I dined well, and recalled in fancy old, youthful Christmases, and pledged mentally many an old friend, and my melancholy was mellowing into a low, sad undertone, when, just as I was raising a glass of wine to my lips, I was startled by a picture at the window-pane. It was a pale, wild, haggard face, in a great cloud of black hair, pressed against the glass. As I looked, it vanished. With a strange thrill at my heart, which my lips mocked with a derisive sneer, I finished the wine and set down the glass. It was, of course, only a beggar-girl that had crept up to the window and stole a glance at the bright scene within; but still the pale face troubled me a little, and threw a fresh shadow on my heart. I filled my glass once more with wine, and was again about to drink, when the face reappeared at the window. It was so white, so thin, with eyes so

large, wild, and hungry-looking, and the black, un-
kempt hair, into which the snow had drifted, formed
so strange and weird a frame to the picture, that I
was fairly startled. Replacing, untasted, the liquor
on the table, I rose and went close to the pane.
The face had vanished, and I could see no object
within many feet of the window. The storm had
increased, and the snow was driving in wild gusts
through the streets, which were empty, save here
and there a hurrying wayfarer. The whole scene
was cold, wild, and desolate, and I could not repress
a keen thrill of sympathy for the child, whoever it
was, whose only Christmas was to watch, in cold and
storm, the rich banquet ungratefully enjoyed by the
lonely bachelor. I resumed my place at the table;
but the dinner was finished, and the wine had no
further relish. I was haunted by the vision at the
window, and began, with an unreasonable irritation
at the interruption, to repeat with fresh warmth my
detestation of holidays. One couldn't even dine
alone on a holiday with any sort of comfort, I declared. On holidays one was tormented by too
much pleasure on one side, and too much misery on
the other. And then, I said, hunting for justification of my dislike of the day, 'How many other
people are, like me, made miserable by seeing the
fullness of enjoyment others possessed!'

"Oh, yes, I know," sarcastically replied the bachelor to a comment of mine ; "of course, all magnanimous, generous, and noble-souled people delight in seeing other people made happy, and are quite content to accept this vicarious felicity. But I, you see, and this dear little girl—"

"Dear little girl!"

"Oh, I forgot," said Bachelor Bluff, blushing a little, in spite of a desperate effort not to do so. "I didn't tell you. Well, it was so absurd! I kept thinking, thinking of the pale, haggard, lonely little girl on the cold and desolate side of the window-pane, and the over-fed, discontented, lonely old bachelor on the splendid side of the window-pane; and I didn't get much happier thinking about it, I can assure you. I drank glass after glass of the wine—not that I enjoyed its flavor any more, but mechanically, as it were, and with a sort of hope thereby to drown unpleasant reminders. I tried to attribute my annoyance in the matter to holidays, and so denounced them more vehemently than ever. I rose once in a while and went to the window, but could see no one to whom the pale face could have belonged.

"At last, in no very amiable mood, I got up, put on my wrappers, and went out; and the first thing I did was to run against a small figure crouching in the doorway. A face looked up quickly at the rough encounter, and I saw the pale features of the window-pane. I was very irritated and angry, and spoke harshly; and then, all at once, I am sure I don't know how it happened, but it flashed upon me that I, of all men, had no right to utter a harsh word to one oppressed with so wretched a Christmas as this poor creature was. I couldn't say another word, but began feeling in my pocket for some money, and then I asked a question or two, and then I don't quite know how it came about—isn't it very warm here?" exclaimed Bachelor Bluff, rising and walking about, and wiping the perspiration from his brow.

"Well, you see," he resumed, nervously, "it was very absurd, but I did believe the girl's story—the old story, you know, of privation and suffering, and all that — and just thought I'd go home with the brat and see if what she said was all true. And then I remembered that all the shops were closed, and not a purchase could be made. I went back and persuaded the steward to put up for me a hamper of provisions, which the half-wild little youngster helped me carry through the snow, dancing with delight all the way.—And isn't this enough?"

"Not a bit, Mr. Bluff. I must have the whole story."

13

" I declare," said Bachelor Bluff, " there's no
whole story to tell. A widow with children in great
need, that was what I found; and they had a feast
that night, and a little money to buy them a loaf and
a garment or two the next day; and they were all
so bright, and so merry, and so thankful, and so
good, that, when I got home that night, I was might-
ily amazed that, instead of going to bed sour at
holidays, I was in a state of great contentment in
regard to holidays. In fact, I was really merry. I
whistled. I sang. I do believe I cut a caper.
The poor wretches I had left had been so merry
over their unlooked-for Christmas banquet that their
spirits infected mine.

" And then I got thinking again. Of course,
holidays had been miserable to me, I said. What
right had a well-to-do, lonely old bachelor hovering
wistfully in the vicinity of happy circles, when all
about there were so many people as lonely as he,
and yet oppressed with want? 'Good Gracious!' I
exclaimed, 'to think of a man complaining of loneliness with thousands of wretches yearning for his
help and comfort, with endless opportunities for work
and company, with hundreds of pleasant and delightful things to do! Just to think of it!' It
put me in a great fury at myself to think of it. I
tried pretty hard to escape from myself, and began

inventing excuses and all that sort of thing, but I
rigidly forced myself to look squarely at my own
conduct. And then I reconciled my conscience by
declaring that, if ever after that day I hated a holiday again, might my holidays end at once and for
ever!

"Did I go and see my *protégés* again? What
a question! Why—well, no matter. If the widow
is comfortable now, it is because she has found a
way to earn without difficulty enough for her few
wants. That's no fault of mine. I would have
done more for her, but she wouldn't let me. But
just let me tell you about New-Year's—the New-
Year's-day that followed the Christmas I've been
describing. It was lucky for me there was another
holiday only a week off. Bless you! I had so
much to do that day that I was completely bewildered, and the hours weren't half long enough.
I did make a few social calls, but then I hurried
them over; and then hastened to my little girl,
whose face had already caught a touch of color;
and she, looking quite handsome in her new frock
and her ribbons, took me to other poor folk, and—
well, that's about the whole story.

"Oh, as to the next Christmas. Well, I didn't
dine alone, as you may guess. It was up three
stairs, that's true, and there was none of that ele-

gance that marked the dinner of the year before; but it was merry, and happy, and bright; it was a generous, honest, hearty, Christmas dinner, that it was, although I do wish the widow hadn't talked so much about the mysterious way a turkey had been left at her door the night before. And Molly —that's the little girl—and I had a rousing appetite. We went to church early; then we had been down to the Five Points to carry the poor outcasts there something for their Christmas dinner; in fact, we had done wonders of work, and Molly was in high spirits, and so the Christmas dinner was a great success.

"Dear me, sir, no! Just as you say. Holidays are not in the least wearisome any more. Plague on it! When a man tells me now that he hates holidays, I find myself getting very wroth. I pin him by the button-hole at once, and tell him my experience. The fact is, if I were at dinner on a holiday, and anybody should ask me for a sentiment, I should say, 'God bless all holidays!'"

THE END.

www.ingramcontent.com/pod-product-compliance
Lightning Source LLC
Chambersburg PA
CBHW020853020726
47497CB00005B/1389